Love's Allegiance

By Linda Shenton Matchett

Love's Allegiance

By Linda Shenton Matchett

Cover Design and author photo by: Wes Matchett

Steamer trunk image: David Nisley. Woman in field image: Ysbrand Cosijn.

ISBN-13: 978-0-9985265-8-4

Published by Shortwave Press

To

Barbara Flaherty

Poet, Visionary, and Best Friend Extraordinaire

April, 1943 Mechanicsburg, PA

Chapter One

"Let's face it, Claire. Marriage isn't in the cards for me." Rochelle

Addams spoke through the hair pins clenched between her lips as she

inspected her image in the mirror and fought to tame her straight brown

hair into victory rolls.

Claire Porter sat cross-legged on the bed filing her nails.

"Nonsense. You're just saying that because you haven't met the right guy

yet."

"No. I'm saying it because it's true. We're just about to graduate

from college. No one is looking my way."

In the distance a train whistle wailed, and Rochelle gestured

toward the darkening sky outside the window. "Hear that? Probably

another troop transport taking the remaining eligible men to combat.

Everyone who's left is either too young or too old. Despite the optimism that this war will be over by Christmas, I have my doubts. Hitler seems determined to take over Europe, and he's not going to give up easily." She shrugged. "I'll be on the other side of thirty at the rate this war is going."

"You're in a dark mood tonight." Claire rose and pulled the navy-blue dress from the back of the chair. She held it in front of herself, then executed several dance steps before stopping behind Rochelle. She cocked her head and met her friend's gaze in the mirror. "It's been months since you and Warren broke up. You need to get back out there."

"I know, but it doesn't matter. Like I said, there's no one to date."

"Perhaps you should join the Pen-Pal Club. A bunch of us get together on Tuesday nights to write letters to servicemen." Claire grinned. "You could meet someone, but you wouldn't have to survive the dreaded first date."

Rochelle chuckled. "They can be awful, can't they?"

"Remember the time Johnny Jenkins took you to the summer carnival? What a disaster." Claire returned the dress to the chair. "You never did get that mustard stain off your white sweater."

"He bought me a new one and apologized every time he saw me before enlisting last year." Rochelle shook her head. "That wasn't the worst of it. Do you remember that we left the fair kind of late, so he decided to take a short cut down some dirt road? The car got stuck in a mud slick, and we had to walk almost three miles to find the nearest pay phone. I was wearing brand-new high heels. My blisters had blisters."

Claire snickered. "Poor Johnny."

"Poor Johnny? Poor me!" Rochelle sighed. "To be honest, it doesn't seem right to think about finding a husband and settling down. Dating seems too frivolous. The country is in a life and death struggle."

"That's exactly the reason you should consider dating or at least writing to some of the boys in the military. We have to go about our daily lives, or the Axis powers will have won. We can't let them make us afraid of the future."

"I'm not afraid. I'm simply being realistic." Rochelle walked to the closet and rummaged for a pair of shoes among the jumble of oxfords, pumps, and flats on the floor. "I want to do something more for the cause, something that makes a difference, but Mother and Daddy have been somewhat of a bore about what I can do. It's bad enough they wouldn't let me board at the university, but they've taking to commenting on everything I do. Not that they have much of a say at my age, but…" She grabbed a pair of peep-toe heels then rose to her full five-foot-ten-inch height, pursed her lips, and looked down her nose. "It's all about reputation, dahling. You mustn't tarnish the family's reputation by doing anything untoward." Rochelle scoffed. "Untoward? What does that even mean? It's like she thinks we're high class or rich. Nothing could be further from the truth."

Claire dropped onto the bed. "My parents are intentionally vague like that. The phrase covers anything they want it to." She inspected her nails then glanced at Rochelle. "We could volunteer somewhere. There are lots of organizations. Surely, girls with our skills and…uh…enthusiasm can find something."

Rochelle laughed and sat beside Claire, pulling her legs up under herself. "That's not exactly the word I'd use to describe you. You seem more eager to pursue marriage to Danny than supporting the cause."

"That's because this stupid war ruined everything. He was going to propose, then he decided we should wait to marry until the fighting is over because he could get called up any time."

"At least he hasn't run off to enlist."

"I wouldn't put it past him." Claire huffed out a loud breath. "Whenever we go out he mentions the latest guy who has joined up."

Rubbing her moist palms on her skirt, Rochelle cleared her throat. "Other than wrecking your plans of matrimony, what do you really think about the war? I mean, I feel like I'm fairly mature, but guys who just got out of high school are going halfway…no…all the way around the world to kill other guys. I can't imagine what that must be like. Why can't men talk things out instead of shooting each other?"

"Goodness, where did this come from?"

Rochelle shrugged. "I've been reading the papers, and the news seems all bad. So many battles. So many casualties. I know what Hitler and Mussolini are doing is terrible, but there's so much death and destruction. How can I support that?"

Claire narrowed her eyes. "That's the kind of stuff those conscientious objectors say. Are you one of them? I thought I knew you better than that."

"No." Rochelle waved her hand in a dismissive gesture. "I'm not a CO, but I can understand where they are coming from. Jesus said 'blessed are the peacemakers.' How do we reconcile war with His words?"

"Don't ask me. I'm no theologian. Have you spoken with Pastor Wynkoop about your thoughts? He might be able to help you." She cocked her head. "I don't suppose you've mentioned this to your parents."

"Heavens, no. Mother may not want me rubbing shoulders with the masses, but she certainly wants me to be seen doing my bit. And I want to do something other than collecting scrap and roll bandages like we've been doing. I'm ready for more than going to classes and studying." She fiddled with the hem of her skirt. "What if I talk to the pastor, and he says something to them?"

"He can't do that. Confidentiality of the pastorate. He can't even tell a judge what you say, right?"

"I don't know. Are conversations with a minister the same as confession with a priest?"

"Hmmm. Maybe."

"It doesn't matter. I think I'll stick with telling my best friend." Rochelle smiled. "She's great at keeping secrets."

Claire pressed her index finger and thumb together, ran them across her lips, then pretended to toss a key over her shoulder. She rubbed her hands over her arms. "We still haven't figured out where we can volunteer. There are posters all over town. Do you have any ideas?"

"Not the WAVES, WAACS, or SPARS." Rochelle grinned. "The uniformed services are stricter than Mother and Daddy. No, thanks."

"We could be Donut Dollies with the Red Cross or boost morale in a USO clubmobile."

"We could."

"Now who's lacking enthusiasm?"

Rochelle giggled. "I just can't see myself riding in a bus bucking and swaying over rutted roads for hours then handing out food in the middle of nowhere. I'm not exactly a whiz in the kitchen."

Claire slapped her forehead and snorted a laugh. "Good point. Neither of us is Betty Crocker. How about being a Gray Lady in one of the VA hospitals? Those boys who come home injured need lots of love and attention."

"If I didn't know better, I'd think you were still trying to fix me up with a date."

"No, but if you're afraid of getting involved with someone you can always ask the head nurse to assign you to the coma ward, so you can work with the unconscious ones."

"Very funny." Rochelle nudged Claire's shoulder, then got up and went to her desk. "You didn't mean to, but you reminded me about an article I read." Brow furrowed in concentration, she shuffled through the stack of papers littering the surface. "Ah ha, here it is." She held up a wrinkled newspaper then paged through it. Finding the article, she laid the broadsheet on the bed and pointed to the one-inch headline: "Mental Hospitals Short Staffed. Volunteers Desperately Needed." I could make a real difference with a job like this."

"A bughouse?" Claire gaped at her. "You've flipped your wig."

"Claire! Don't call it that. Who better to help than people who can't help themselves? Didn't Jesus say we should serve 'the least of these?'

"I don't know, Rochelle. Our education didn't prepare us for a mental hospital."

"The article says they will train us, but it's not like we'd be giving out medication. There are lots of positions. Cooks, launderers, clerks, and ward attendants."

"You *are* serious."

"Yes. And you should come with me. There are facilities all over the U.S. We could get out of Mechanicsburg."

"Count me out, sister. If Danny gets called up, I don't want to miss any of the time we have left. I support your decision, but I can't go." Claire tapped her finger on her chin and chuckled. "Smart girl, a mental hospital is the last place you have to worry about finding a boyfriend."

April 1943, Baltimore, MD

Chapter Two

Black clouds swirled overhead as the sky wept buckets of tears.

How fitting. Irwin Terrell lowered his head, and water rolled off the brim

of his black fedora. Pastor Croft read the twenty-third Psalm, his sonorous

voice rumbling like thunder. Beside Irwin, Father stood ramrod straight,

his face a pale mask of pain and loss. The space around the gravesite was

packed with mourners, evidence of Mother's graciousness and loving

kindness, to friends as well as strangers.

A pit formed in Irwin's stomach. He should have bypassed the cup

of coffee he gulped down before the service. Pressing a hand against his

middle, he shifted, and his shoes squished in the muddy grass. Urns of

bedraggled flowers stood to one side, their syrupy fragrance mingling with

the earthy scent emanating from the gaping hole next to the coffin.

He glanced at his wristwatch. Three o'clock. Years of farming had sharpened his ability to use the heavens as a timepiece, but the sun hidden behind the black clouds rendered his skills useless.

Father cleared his throat, and Irwin placed his hand on the older man's shoulder. Tension pulsed beneath his fingers. Muted weeping from the attendees punctuated Pastor Croft's homily.

"Shirley Terrell was a special woman. Gifted with the ability to set others at ease, she anticipated their needs. Small in physical stature, she was a giant in the faith. I can tell you from personal experience that she never met a stranger. Within moments of becoming your pastor many years ago, she welcomed me with a smile and a pie."

An affirming laugh swept through the crowd.

"Sounds like you know exactly what I mean. I figure she's in heaven doing the same thing right now. We will miss her here on earth, but our lives are fuller for having known her. You are a loving congregation, and I know you will walk beside her husband, Arthur, and her son, Irwin, as we grieve the loss of our fine sister in Christ. Let us pray."

Irwin blinked away the tears that threatened to fall. Not that he was typically sentimental, but Father's expectations of him didn't include crying, even at a funeral. Emotions by men were to be avoided at best, but handled in private if necessary. On the other hand, Mother had cried at sappy cards and happily-ever-after movies, especially anything that featured Jimmy Stewart. She had alternately been proud and disappointed when the lanky star put his career on hold last year to enlist in the Army Air Force.

Pastor Croft's "amen" faded, and the sea of umbrellas undulated as well-wishers approached Father to shake hands and offer condolences. The crowd finally dissipated, and the last car pulled away from the avenue that circled the cemetery.

Irwin climbed into the driver's seat and turned the key in the ignition. Father slipped in beside him as the engine roared to life then settled into a throaty purr. He pulled away from the curb and eased the vehicle along the macadam, passing acres of tombstones and mausoleums, finally turning onto Wilkens Avenue.

Silence filled the Packard, and Irwin stole a glance at Father while threading his way through the city. Thanks to gas rationing, traffic was light, and they returned home in short order. Trudging up the stairs and into the empty house, they settled in the living room.

Irwin twisted the knob on the radio. Static crackled.

"Not just yet, son."

"What?"

"Don't turn on the radio. I have something to discuss with you."

"Can't it wait?"

"No. If it weren't for your mother's illness, we'd have had this conversation months ago."

Irwin shut off the radio and raised his eyebrows. Leaning against the table, he crossed his arms. "This sounds serious. Haven't we had enough of that today?"

Father gestured to the chocolate-brown, upholstered chair by the fireplace that Mother used at the end of each day, her knitting needles clacking or darning needle flashing.

Skirting her seat, he lowered himself onto the matching chair and laced his fingers. "I'm listening."

The mantle clock chimed, and the muscle in Father's jaw twitched, the only sign of his coiled emotions.

Irwin sighed. The man would make his point when he was ready.

"Irwin, losing your mother has brought me face-to-face with my own mortality. Yes, she was taken from us because of sickness, but I'm not getting any younger."

"Father—"

"Hear me out."

"Of course."

"You know Mother and I had you late in life. I'm nearly seventy years old. I love this farm, but nearly four thousand acres and the associated staff are a lot to manage. And the constantly changing government regulations in addition to dealing with our regular suppliers and distributors is wearing. Earnest handles most of the paperwork, but there are endless decisions to be made. Each night I'm more tired than the day before. Eventually, it will all pass to you, and when it does, you should have a wife standing beside you…a family. It's time for you to give serious consideration to marriage."

Irwin sighed. It had been months since Father had broached the subject. Why did he have to address it today of all days? Why did everyone think he needed to be married to be happy or productive? Father had enough employees to run things efficiently. In fact, the foreman had been in charge since before Irwin was born.

"Father, I know you mean well. You and mom had a marriage few people are blessed to enjoy, but I'm not sure a bride is in my future. I'm content being single. And frankly, as much as I like working with you, I'm not a farmer. Even you must admit that my abilities will never be what they should to keep this property producing. I can't see myself being here for the rest of my life. I want to help people directly.

"This property has been in the family for five generations. You can't walk away from it."

"Don't act so shocked. We've spoken of this before. I told you after last year's harvest that I wanted to look for a different line of work. I foolishly thought the war would be over by now, but Hitler and Mussolini are not giving up easily. The conflict is going to be long and ugly."

He reached into his pocket and pulled out a folded sheet of paper. "I received notification that my CO status has been approved."

Father slumped against the arm of the sofa and rubbed his forehead. "You went through with the application? Being an only son and working on a farm would have given you exemptions from service. Is this because of that church you've been attending?"

"No, but I do agree with their philosophy. Jesus was quite clear when He said, 'Blessed are the peacemakers.' We're to love our enemies and turn the other cheek."

"What about all the times in the Old Testament that God had the Israelites combat their enemies?"

Irwin shrugged. "I'm not going to argue theology with you, Father. My convictions are firm. I don't believe that God has called me to serve in combat, but I do want to do my part."

"Are you prepared to deal with the ridicule? The treatment you'll receive from those who know you? That Mennonite boy two streets over is a CO, and everyone shunned him until he left."

Irwin stared at his father. "Are you ashamed of me?"

Father blew out a deep breath. "No. I'm proud of you for sticking to your principles. It sounds like you've given them a lot of prayer and thought."

"I appreciate your support. I don't want to cause you any trouble." Irwin pocketed the notice. "Normally, I'd be assigned to one of the soil conservation camps to start my service, but there is a mental hospital in Delaware that is critically short of staff. Selective Service has agreed to let me work there. I'm to report for duty in three weeks."

"A mental hospital? You're not a doctor. Why would they send you there?"

"Because I asked them to, and the facility is in dire straits. Men are enlisting and being called up daily. The hospital's patient-to-attendant ratio is dangerously high. I will be trained how to care for the men— something important—not wasting my time on some government project dreamed up to hide us away. They're ashamed of COs and want to keep us out of the public eye."

"That's harsh—"

"But true. Even though COs are part of the Selective Service, we don't receive wages. What does that say about their feelings with regard to our service?" Irwin rose and finger-combed his hair. He paced in front of the fireplace. "Look, I know you mean well by laying out my life, and as my father you have every right, but I want to decide what's right for me. And getting married and owning a farm isn't in my plans."

"It was at one time. At least, the marriage part."

"Well, that was before Gertrude left me at the altar. I'm not ready to subject myself to that possibility again. At least, not yet. I want to explore other possibilities, and the war is giving me an opportunity to do that. I like the idea of serving those less fortunate, those who are struggling to make sense of the world. People fear the mentally ill. I want to show them acceptance and care." He stopped in front of Father. "I know you want the farm to stay in the family, but would you consider giving it to Mr. Miller, the foreman? With all the years he's worked here, he deserves to be considered."

"I'm saddened by your decision to leave the farm, but I know this life is not for everyone. I'd hoped you'd change your mind. I'll think about your request with regard to Henry Miller, but you're thirty years old. It's time to settle down and start a family. You must realize that."

"No, I don't. There's no formula about when a man should marry."

"There is a young woman out there that God is preparing for you." Father smiled, and his eyes glistened with unshed tears. "I'm going to find her, and you're going to be as happy as your mother and I were."

Irwin clenched his hands into fists and stuffed them into his pockets. The day he was to report to Delaware couldn't come soon enough.

Chapter Three

Rochelle climbed to her feet and brushed clumps of soil off the knees of her coveralls. She rotated her shoulders and flexed her fingers inside the bulky canvas gloves. With a grin, she waved at the petite woman planting seeds in the adjoining garden plot. The city had requisitioned several parks and divided them into victory gardens for those who didn't have enough land to create fields of their own, and she loved the opportunity to escape the house to toil in the dirt.

Mother had initially frowned upon the denim outfit, but after the Women's Land Army made wearing them popular, she quit complaining. Not that she'd be caught dead in one herself, but she'd purchased the Hollywood pattern and material, and had her seamstress make two for Rochelle.

Overhead, the sun played hide-and-seek with white, puffy clouds giving some relief to the relentless heat. The winter had been mild, and it seemed summer was going to be early.

Pulling a handkerchief from her pocket, Rochelle blotted the perspiration from her face. She removed her wide-brimmed sailor hat and fanned herself for a few moments then returned the straw hat to her head. She surveyed her work and blew out a deep breath. Precise rows of rich, brown earth stretched in front of her. Her body ached from top to bottom, but the pain would be worth it when the family had access to fresh vegetables throughout the season.

"Two more rows to go. This garden isn't going to finish itself." Rochelle stuffed the handkerchief into her pocket and knelt on the ground. She picked out stray rocks and tossed them to the side then poked string bean seeds into the soil every three inches as she crawled along the ridge of dirt.

Twenty minutes later she reached the end of the row and looked up. Near the entrance to the park, a lone black Packard sedan gleamed in the sunshine. Who could afford such a fancy vehicle? She shielded her eyes with a gloved hand and searched among the plots for someone who might belong to the pristine vehicle.

"There you are." Rochelle sat back on her haunches as a lanky, bespectacled man with graying hair picked his way through the cordoned-off sections of land. His wool, pewter-colored suit, crisp white shirt, and muted-gray tie contrasted with the gardeners' denim and cotton outfits. She snickered. Dressed to the nines, and the only man among dozens of women.

Two plots away, Maria Cooke rose. With one hand on her hip, she patted her bandana-covered hair with the other, and produced an ingratiating smile. She dipped and swayed more than the five o'clock train into Philadelphia.

Rochelle rolled her eyes and huffed a sigh. Neither the gentleman nor Maria were her business and gawking at the stranger wouldn't complete her chores. She glanced at the watch pinned to the bodice of the coveralls and returned to the ground. If she didn't pick up her speed, she'd miss the next bus. Shoving a trowel into the soil, she breathed in the pungent aroma.

Poke a hole. Plant a seed. Poke a hole. Plant a seed. Scoot forward.

The hypnotic rhythm of the task soothed her scattered thoughts, and she hummed the latest Jimmy Dorsey tune. Bobbing her head, she dropped the tiny beans in time with the music.

"You have a lovely voice, Miss Addams."

Rochelle's heart skittered, and her head whipped toward the voice. The well-dressed man stood on the other side of the row. She scrambled to rise, but lost her balance and fell onto her backside with a thud. Her face warmed.

He extended a well-manicured hand, his eyes dark with concern. "Are you all right, miss?"

She nodded and stood, ignoring his assistance, then brushed off the dirt she imagined clung to her clothing. "Yes, I just injured my pride. You startled me."

"Forgive me."

"That's okay. No need to apologize. I wasn't blaming you." She frowned. "Wait. How do you know my name?"

He glanced behind her. "One of the ladies pointed you out."

"Of course. Maria Cooke. She knows…and tells everything. Did she give you my whole life story or the abbreviated version?"

"Well—" His face flamed.

Rochelle hiked a shoulder. "That answers my question, but you have me at a disadvantage. You know all about me, but I have no idea who you are."

His color deepened. "I'm making a mess of things, aren't I? Let's start over." He put his heels together and bowed. "Allow me to introduce myself, Miss Addams. My name is Earnest Young. I work for the Terrell family in Baltimore, Maryland. They are related to you by a distant relative who came from England shortly before the American Revolution, a Jeremiah Griffin. Mr. Terrell sent me to discuss an important proposition with you."

Huh? Jeremiah Griffin? "It's nice to meet you, but are you sure I'm the right person? I've never heard of your employer or this Griffin guy from England. And as far as I'm aware, we don't have any family from Baltimore or anywhere else in Maryland, for that matter."

"Your parents are Bertrand and Violet Addams, correct?"

"Yes, but perhaps there's another couple by that name."

"Highly unlikely, and certainly not in Mechanicsburg, Pennsylvania. You are the woman I'm seeking."

Rochelle caught movement in her peripheral vision. Several of the women clustered together staring at her and Mr. Young. Perfect. How much had the ladies heard?

Mr. Young followed her gaze and pressed his lips together. "Perhaps we should continue this conversation in a more private location. May I offer you a ride home, so we can discuss the offer with your father?"

"I don't normally get into cars with strangers, but you seem on the up-and-up. And I definitely want to get away from the neighborhood gossips. I don't live far, but judging from that vehicle of yours I'm assuming gasoline supply isn't a problem for your employer."

"Mr. Terrell doesn't purchase more than his fair share, and he secured the necessary permissions and stamps for me to make this journey."

"Good to know he's on the straight and narrow, too."

Mr. Young offered his arm, and she grinned before tucking her hand in to the crook of his elbow. "May as well give them as much to talk about as possible." She tossed her trowel in the bucket with her other tools, picked it up, then straightened her spine and sauntered to the car as if she were in evening wear and pearls. "How in the world did you find me, Mr. Young? I'm not exactly at home receiving visitors."

"As you surmised, Mr. Terrell is a man of means. He was able to secure the services of a private investigator who found your family."

"A PI? Like Philo Vance?"

"Something like that." Mr. Young chuckled. "But not as stylish."

"More like Sam Spade, maybe. How about that?"

Mr. Young opened the door to the sedan's back seat and gestured for Rochelle to climb inside. She lowered herself onto the supple tan leather seat and cringed. "I'm going to get dirt all over your nice car. Maybe I should take the bus, and you can meet me at home."

"The seats will be fine. You sit back and enjoy being chauffeured. I'll have you home in no time."

She rubbed her palms along the buttery surfaces of the interior. The day was nothing like she'd planned. Would she have time to tell Claire that she'd exchanged bean planting for a chauffeured ride in a luxury car before Maria spread the word around town?

Mr. Young slid into the driver's seat. The engine roared to life, and he pulled away from the curb. She waved at the gardeners who hadn't moved. Gaping, they seemed too stunned to return her farewell.

Rochelle leaned back and sighed. This beat a trip on the bus by a landslide. The vehicle rumbled along the macadam, and she watched the brick-and-glass store-fronts give way to brick-and-wood homes standing shoulder to shoulder.

Fifteen minutes later, Mr. Young parked the car in front of the tiny brick row house that had been in her family for three generations.

She waited until Mr. Young opened her door. As her feet hit the pavement, her brother, Leonard, limped toward the vehicle, his face a mixture of suspicion and anger. Leave it to him to overreact and assume the worst.

Before he could dress her down in the front yard, she held up her hand, palm toward him. "Hello, Leonard. This is Mr. Earnest Young, and he's driven a very long way with a message for Father from our relatives. Is he home?"

Leonard's mouth worked, but nothing came out. He must have realized how rude he appeared because a smile appeared on his lips, and he extended his hand. "Welcome to our home, Mr. Young. I'm Leonard Addams."

The two men shook hands, and Leonard shrugged. "Father has a civil defense meeting. He should be home in about thirty minutes. Would you like to come inside for refreshments? I believe we have iced tea and gingerbread if you're hungry."

"I'd prefer to wait until we've had our conversation, if you don't mind. But I will come inside."

Leonard led them up the stairs and into the house where they seated themselves in the parlor. Loathe to leave their guest unattended with her brother, Rochelle decided not to change her clothes. Mother wouldn't be happy, but it seemed the lesser of two evils.

Mr. Young turned to Leonard and cleared his throat. "Let me set your mind at ease, Mr. Addams. As I told your sister, I work for Mr. Arthur Terrell. His wife recently passed away after a brief illness, and his son, Irwin, is their only child. Mr. Terrell is interested in developing a relationship between your two families."

"What sort of relationship?" Leonard crossed his arms, his expression mulish.

"I'll review the details with your father. Meanwhile, I've brought gifts for all of you." He lifted the lid on the cordovan leather briefcase he'd carried in from the car. He handed Leonard a mahogany box, then passed two Tiffany-Blue jeweler's boxes to Rochelle. "Please, open them. These are a sampling of the items I've brought."

Leonard cracked the box, and his eyes widened. He withdrew a sterling silver fountain pen and matching mechanical pencil. "Thank you, sir, but I can't accept these. They are too much."

"There are no strings attached to the gifts. Mr. Terrell wishes you to have them no matter what the outcome of today's visit."

"Um…all right. Thank you." He returned the writing instruments to the box then stroked the intricately carved patterns on the lid. "What did you get, Chelley?"

Nibbling her lower lip, Rochelle swallowed. He hadn't called her that in ages. Not since he'd returned home from the battle that took his leg. The hinges on the box squeaked as she lifted the top and exposed a pair of emerald earrings encircled with diamonds. Why in the world…? She could at least be polite. "They're lovely, Mr. Young. Thank you."

He smiled and nodded. "You're very welcome, Miss Addams. There is a matching bracelet in the other box."

Rochelle narrowed her eyes. Why would Mr. Terrell send such expensive gifts? A bribe? An inducement? Whatever the reason, there was no way she'd let the loot sway her. "Mr. Terrell's proposition must be a doozy, Mr. Young."

Chapter Four

The sun warmed Irwin's back as he bent over the unwieldy boat motor laying on the plywood he'd propped on a pair of sawhorses. He could have taken the engine to a mechanic, but he enjoyed doing the work himself. He tightened his grip on the crescent wrench and tried to loosen the stubborn bolt. The tool shot from his sweat-slicked palm and landed on the ground with a clatter. Pressing his lips together, he wiped his hands on his pants.

Father approached. "We can pay to have that done, son."

"Yes, but I enjoy the work. If things were different, I might have chosen to be an automobile mechanic." He retrieved the errant implement and tucked it into his pocket. "I've seen you perform tasks you don't need to."

Father nodded. "True. Sometimes I miss the simplicity of our lives before the farm became so successful as a commercial enterprise, when it was just you, your mother, and me."

"I can understand that. You're responsible for a lot of lives which must be a heavy burden."

"It can be, but God has blessed us mightily, so it's only right that I pass along our abundance."

Irwin tugged at his ear "You're a good man, Father. I've learned a lot from you over the years, other than farming."

"It's a father's job to train his son. Why the sentimentality?"

Irwin shrugged. "I'm going to be leaving soon for who knows how long. You're uncomfortable with this kind of conversation, but I wanted you to know."

Father shifted from foot to foot. "Just because I don't want to talk about emotions doesn't mean I don't feel them." He cleared his throat. "I'm going to miss you and not because of the work you do around here.

I'm proud of you, son, of the man you've become. For choosing to walk a path that isn't popular, that ironically some consider contentious."

"Thank you for believing in me. Word is already out. I guess old Barney at the telegraph office doesn't think confidentiality is part of his job. When I was at the service station getting supplies for this, I got a few snide remarks tossed at me. It seems people think I don't care that our boys are in harm's way. Others intimated that I'm a coward or trying to take it easy." Irwin sighed. "I do care about the servicemen. But I can't go against my convictions."

"Sometimes people are going to believe what they want no matter how much you try to explain a different point of view. And they're afraid. Afraid for their families and themselves, and your mindset may seem to belittle their sacrifices." He held out his hand for the wrench. "Let me help you."

"It hurts enough when a stranger is rude, but when friends are unforgiving…well…it's been difficult." Irwin blew out a deep breath then gave him the tool. He pointed to the unmoving bolt. "See if you can get that stubborn thing to turn."

Father inspected the motor then leaned over and began to wield the wrench. "You still feeling good about the position in Delaware with the hospital, despite people's ill will?" His voice was muffled. "Perhaps you'll be in danger after all."

"I've been praying about the assignment, and I get the sense it's what I'm supposed to be doing. Maybe the job will change the course of my life after the war, or maybe it's only where God wants me for the time being. But Jesus' words about 'the least of these' keep coming to my mind. I haven't received another letter from the facility, so I'll find out more when I get there, but I don't think I need to fear the work...or the patients. Yes, perhaps some are violent, but I believe a kind word and acceptance of them will go a long way to helping them."

"If you say so, but there's a reason psychologists go to school for a long time. Physical wounds can be sewn or patched. Mental wounds aren't that obvious and more difficult to repair, or so it would seem."

"I'll leave the cures to the doctors." Irwin rocked back on his heels. "I'm looking forward to the change in scenery. I hear Delaware is beautiful."

"I was in Delaware once. Many years ago." The bolt shifted, and he grunted. "Your grandfather claimed he heard about a new strain of corn, and he sent me to investigate. Turned out to be an excuse to get me there." A distant look filled Father's eyes. "Your mother was visiting her aunt and uncle, and he knew that. Apparently, he'd been trying to get us together for months, and nothing worked. Mixed-up schedules, traveling, and the growing season all served to keep us apart."

Irwin raised his eyebrows. "You've never shared that story before. I thought you met Mother here at church."

"No." A soft laugh rumbled in his chest. "We got to know one another through the church, but the first time I laid eyes on her was a sun-filled afternoon, much like today. She and her cousin were sitting on the porch shelling peas. Her hair gleamed in the breeze, and when she giggled her smile lit up her face like a beacon." Father hiked one shoulder. "I was smitten. Just like your grandfather thought I'd be. Of course, the more I got to know her gentle and caring spirit, the more I loved her."

"Why—"

Tires crunched over gravel, and Irwin pivoted toward the noise. The Packard shimmied as it rolled around the circular driveway. Earnest was at the wheel, and a young woman sat in the back seat. Irwin rubbed his stubbled jaw. A new employee? Why would Father's secretary be chauffeuring staff?

Nodding his head, and his hand at a half wave, his father didn't seem surprised.

"Father?"

The vehicle lumbered to a stop, and Earnest got out. He opened the back door then extended his hand to the passenger. She gripped his fingers with slender ones of her own and slid from the car.

Irwin blinked. Chestnut-brown hair fell below the girl's shoulders. A tentative smile formed on her lips beneath porcelain cheeks and dark eyes. Her green dress, the color of new moss, accentuated her lithe figure.

The skirt fluttered in the breeze, exposing well-shaped legs. Her face pinked as she attempted to tame the unruly garment.

Earnest bowed to the girl and gestured toward Father who wore a satisfied smile. They approached, her steps tentative. Irwin straightened his shoulders and wished he wore something other than dirty work clothes. Even his scuffed shoes had seen better days. With his handkerchief he rubbed his face, hoping to create some semblance of cleanliness. He caught sight of his grease-stained fingers and cringed. Not a great first impression.

Wait. Why was he worried about any sort of impression? He was leaving. Soon. It didn't matter what she thought.

Yeah. Try telling that to his heart that skipped more than a few beats at her appearance.

"Irwin?" Father nudged his shoulder.

"Hmm?" Great. He'd been caught staring like a toddler in a candy shop.

"Earnest made good time. They're early. I'd hoped to tell you about her, but—"

"Who is she?" Irwin tilted his head. "Why is your secretary carting around a new employee?"

Father sniggered. "She's not staff, son. She's family. Distant family, but family all the same. Her name is Rochelle Addams, and she's lovely. I can see from your expression you agree. That's good."

A knot formed in Irwin's stomach, and the muscles in his neck stiffened. "What's going on?"

"I've arranged for Rochelle to stay with us until you leave, so you can get to know each other."

"You—"

"She'll make an excellent bride."

Chapter Five

Rochelle held her skirts in place and followed Mr. Young toward

the men he'd indicated were Mr. Terrell and his son. Besides wearing

nearly identical work clothes, the men had the same build, the same facial

structure, and coloring.

The pair had obviously been repairing an engine, and their

camaraderie seemed to evaporate moments after she stepped from the

vehicle. In fact, Irwin wore an expression of suspicion mixed with

confusion. Had Father withheld the reason for her visit?

Mr. Terrell stepped forward and dipped his head then held up his

hands. "I'd offer to shake your hand, Miss Addams, but as you can see

that wouldn't be appropriate. I apologize for our appearance. Your arrival wasn't expected for another hour or so." He looked at Mr. Young with a bemused smile.

"We were able to get an earlier start than anticipated, sir."

"Quite all right, Earnest. We're pleased to see you, Miss Addams. This is my son, Irwin. Irwin, Miss Rochelle Addams. She's come from Pennsylvania."

"Uh, it's nice to meet you." Irwin spoke through stiff lips.

"Thank you. I'm glad to be here. Mr. Young is a wonderful driver, but the trip to Maryland took longer than expected. The scenery is beautiful, but even that got tedious after the first couple of hours. I may have dozed off." She clapped a hand over her mouth. They must think her a ninny, prattling on like she did.

Mr. Terrell smiled, and the skin around his eyes crinkled. "Understandable. Would you like to freshen up? You could lie down for a bit. Later, Irwin can give you a tour of the property."

She glanced at Irwin who stood with his arms wrapped around his middle, his face unreadable. Patting her hair, she said, "I wouldn't mind changing my clothes into something more appropriate for a walk around the grounds."

"Excellent. Earnest, please show Miss Addams to her room and where the parlor is, so she can meet us there."

"Yes, sir." Mr. Young returned to the car and pulled her suitcases from the trunk.

The older man nudged his son who gave her a curt nod before pulling out a metal tool from his pocket.

Rochelle blinked back tears and hurried to catch up with the secretary who walked toward the stately brick home. Perhaps traveling almost one hundred miles to consider marrying a man she'd never met wasn't her best decision.

She stumbled on the cobblestone walk that led to the dwelling, and her face warmed. Nearly a dozen windows on each floor seemed to laugh at her in the sunlight. Ducking her head, she approached the ornate entrance flanked by oak trees that soared high above the slate roof. Manicured gardens dotted the front yard. The property was nothing like she imagined when Mr. Young indicated the Terrells operated a large farm. His gifts should have been her first clue that nothing would be as expected.

Her footsteps echoed in the expansive foyer. A chandelier sparkled overhead casting rainbows of light onto pristine beige walls. A gilt-framed portrait of a serious-looking man in nineteenth-century attire hung to her right. Across the room, a smaller oil painting of Mr. Terrell and an attractive, dark-haired woman graced the wall. His wife, no doubt.

"This way, Miss Addams." Mr. Young hesitated at the bottom of the stairs.

"I'm sorry." Rochelle hurried forward. "The artwork caught my attention."

"No need to apologize." He jerked his head toward the man in the picture. "That's Mr. Terrell's great-great-great grandfather. He makes a imposing figure."

"He seems rather stern. Is that a family trait?"

"Irwin will warm up. Just give it time."

She nodded, and the tightness in her chest eased. Was Mr. Young an ally she could count on? She would have preferred another woman with whom she could confide.

They ascended to the second floor, their tread muffled by the thick carpet on the steps. About halfway down the hallway, they entered a large, bright room decorated in shades of yellow. The four-poster, cherry-wood bed and matching nightstands and dresser gleamed. Fortunately, landscapes and still-life paintings accented the room rather than judgmental-looking ancestors.

"I'll send one of the maids up to help you unpack. To find the parlor, go back down the stairs and turn to your left. It's the first door on the right."

"Please don't send anyone. I'm used to taking care of myself."

"As you wish, Miss Addams, but if you remain, you'll need to adjust to having staff handle the mundane, day-to-day matters."

"Maybe, but for today…"

"Yes, miss. I understand." He pointed to a buzzer on the wall near the bed. "Should you change your mind, press that, and someone will arrive to help you." He bowed and slipped out of the room, closing the door.

Tears threatened, and Rochelle blew out a deep breath. How life had changed in the past two days. She made quick work of putting away her clothes in the cedar-lined drawers before washing her face and changing into a floral, cotton dress and a pair of flats. She inspected her image in the free-standing, full-length mirror while she brushed her hair and frowned. Her eyes were dull with fatigue. No wonder Irwin seemed put off by her appearance.

Female voices sounded outside her door, and she froze.

"Did you see the girl who arrived with Mr. Young? She doesn't seem the farm type to me."

"Not everyone is as they seem. That Gertrude woman turned out to be difficult and selfish, nothing like we thought. And what she did to Mr. Irwin, well, it was a real shame."

"I guess time will tell."

"It's too bad…"

The voices faded, and Rochelle yanked open the door. She peeked down the hall. Two young girls dressed in maid's uniforms turned the corner out of sight. Who was Gertrude, and what had she done to Irwin?

A clock chimed from below, and Rochelle glanced at her watch. She'd taken too long. Tossing the hairbrush onto the bed, she closed the door and headed downstairs.

Deep voices filtered from the room as she approached the parlor. Her feet slowed, and a flock of hummingbirds seemed to take flight in her stomach. She pressed a hand against her abdomen and forced herself to keep moving. Just before entering, she stiffened her spine, and lifted her chin, then pinned on a smile.

Mr. Terrell rose. He'd changed into clean slacks and shirt, his hair slicked with Brylcreem. "Miss Addams, you look refreshed. I will leave you in Irwin's good hands while I make some important telephone calls."

She wilted. "Oh. I thought you'd be joining us." Great. Now she'd be alone with the man who seemed to want to be anywhere but with her. Well, if he wasn't going to make it easy on her, she wouldn't give him an inch.

"I'm sure the two of you will manage." He glanced at Irwin who also wore fresh clothing. "Try not to tire our guest. Dinner is at six o'clock." He marched out the doorway, and silence descended.

Rochelle waited, her hands clasped in front of her. She surveyed the finely appointed room decorated in shades of peach and coral. The furniture was exquisite yet inviting, the artwork accentuating the knick-knacks and décor.

Nibbling on the inside of her cheek, she watched Irwin from under lowered lashes.

He finally seemed resigned to his situation and gestured to the ivory-colored sofa. "Would you sit down, Miss Addams? I'd like to clear up a couple of things first."

"Certainly." She sank onto the silken cushion, and it cradled her travel-weary body. She tried not to moan.

Irwin lowered himself beside her, rubbed hands on his pants, then crossed his arms. He huffed a loud sigh. "Look, I don't know what Father told you to get you to visit, but I'm not in the market for a wife. This whole thing is his idea. I've got my orders from Selective Service and will head to Delaware next week. I'd be happy to show you the farm, but there's no reason for you to stay." He narrowed his eyes and leaned back.

She studied him for a long moment until his gaze shifted. Not wanting to give him the satisfaction of any sort of emotional response, she kept her face expressionless and her voice even. "Your father told me the invitation was from him and not you, and that you would be upset when you discovered what he'd done. Should we decide to move forward with this arrangement of getting to know each other to determine if we're suitable, then he will see to it that I'm considered for one of the positions available at the mental hospital."

Irwin opened his mouth, and she raised her hand. "Before you protest, I want you to know that days before your father approached me, I saw a newspaper article about the need for staff in hospitals across the country. I had already decided to apply when Mr. Young arrived with the…ah…proposition. So whether you agree or not, I plan to ask your father to make an inquiry on my behalf."

His mouth gaped into a perfect O, and she refrained from grinning. Apparently, Mr. I-don't-need-a-wife-and-I've-got-my-orders wasn't as self-assured as he appeared. Whether they moved forward with an *agreement* or not, it might be fun to keep him off kilter.

Chapter Six

Irwin sighed as Earnest braked in front of Shady Hills Hospital. He glanced at Rochelle who sat next to him in the back seat in silence, her face a picture of serenity. How could she be so calm when his stomach buzzed in anticipation? Or was she so adept at hiding her feelings that he would never know her true thoughts?

After hours of discussion, they'd agreed to a trial courtship, and the days passed quickly while they prepared to leave for the hospital. Time for leisure was minimal, but they'd enjoyed a picnic by the harbor and a couple of walks around the farm. But he still knew very little about her.

He stepped out of the car then circled the vehicle and opened her door. Leaning down, he extended his hand, and she grasped his fingers.

Warmth stole up his arm at her touch. Her face flushed, and she pressed her lips together as she stood. Had she felt the connection, too?

Earnest retrieved their luggage from the trunk and set it on the ground. "Would you like assistance getting settled, sir?"

"No thanks. I can handle the bags. Or would you like a break before getting back on the road." Irwin grinned. "As if carting my bags up a flight of stairs is a break."

Father's secretary glanced at his watch and shook his head. "I'd best be going. There are stops I need to make on the way, so if you're sure you're okay…"

"Absolutely." Irwin smiled at Rochelle. "Miss Addams and I are quite capable of getting settled on our own, aren't we?"

"Yes." She rushed forward and hugged Earnest. "Thank you for everything, Mr. Young. You've been swell."

The stalwart man's face reddened, and his eyes closed as he endured her embrace. "'Tis quite all right, miss. Nothing out of the ordinary, to be sure. Just doing my job."

She released him and patted his arm. "I don't think so. You're not all memos and inkwells, Mr. Young, no matter what you want me to believe."

He chuckled then said, "Good luck to you, Miss Addams, but you won't need it. Those boys will be lucky to have you."

"That's nice of you to say. Have a safe trip home." Rochelle picked up her train case and the smallest suitcase and squinted at the entrance. "I suppose we should start there."

Earnest waved at Rochelle with a broad smile then got behind the wheel. Since when did the man wave to anyone in the family?

Irwin loaded the remaining bags into his arms.

Rochelle marched up the granite steps and held the door for him. He squeezed through the opening then set down his load.

A blonde-haired woman who appeared to be their age sat behind the reception desk. She looked up from typing and beamed. "You must be Mr. Terrell and Miss Addams. We've been expecting you. I can't tell you how pleased we are that you've decided to join us."

Rochelle smoothed her skirts. "Thank you for your kind welcome. I've been so nervous because I wasn't sure what to expect. Being a hospital, I thought everyone might be a bit stuffy. Or at least on the clinical side, if you know what I mean. It's nice to be greeted with a friendly smile. Your campus is beautiful. I love the stone buildings, and trees and flowers are everywhere. Being close to the ocean—" She glanced at Irwin and frowned. "I'm doing it again." She turned back to the receptionist. "Please forgive me. I'm a bit of a chatterbox when I'm anxious."

"Not need to apologize. I'll get one of the orderlies to show you to your lodging. Lunch is at noon sharp, and after that you'll meet with Dr. O'Dwyer, the hospital superintendent. How does that sound?"

"Wonderful. I'm famished."

Irwin pinched the bridge of his nose. Rochelle was warm and bubbly with others, yet alternately awkward and standoffish with him. What could he do to change the way she acted when in his company?

The woman lifted the telephone receiver, pressed a couple of buttons, and then spoke a few words. Within moments, a lanky man perhaps fifty years old with grizzled beard appeared. His black hair stuck out in several places. He nodded to the receptionist then gestured to a flight of stairs Irwin hadn't noticed. He took two suitcases from Irwin in large hands. "Follow me, and we'll get you tucked in."

They ascended two flights of stairs, making their way to the third floor. Irwin's arms ached, and the baggage got heavier with each step. What had Rochelle packed? The older man seemed unaffected by the climb, and Irwin's face warmed. Would the orderly think he was a sissy? How would the other staff treat him once they knew about his status? Fortunately, there would be other COs at the facility.

The orderly opened a door to a tiny room that held one bed, a dresser, and a ladder-back chair. "This is where you'll be, miss. Which of these bags are yours?"

Rochelle pointed to the suitcases in Irwin's arms.

The man glowered and set down the bags he'd carried up. Stepping back, he crossed his arms, and said, "You can take them from here, *sir.*" Distain colored the title.

Irwin sighed, put Rochelle's bags near her dresser, and then lifted his suitcases. He followed the orderly who strode down the hallway.

Footsteps sounded behind him, and he turned. Rochelle trotted toward him. "Let me see which room you're in, then we can walk the grounds before lunch. I'd like to explore…that is, if you don't mind."

His heart skittered. "I'd enjoy that. I thought perhaps you'd had enough of my company."

A crease appeared between her eyebrows, and her face pinked. "Why would you think that?"

Great. She'd finally seemed to want to be around him, and he'd hurt her feelings. He needed to stop acting like a bear with a sore paw, or no one would want to spend time with him, including the patients.

He blew out a deep breath. "I—"

"Are you coming? I ain't got all day." The orderly stood at the end of the hall, hands on his hips, lips twisted.

"Sorry. Irwin headed toward the man with Rochelle on his heels. "Seems I'm upsetting everyone today. Not an auspicious start to my assignment, is it?"

"Let's get your things put away, and we can start over." Rochelle rolled her eyes. "Without the chaperone."

He sped up, his steps light. She didn't think he was a total boar, so he had a chance. A chance at being someone she could look up to.

Fifteen minutes later they were outside and sauntering along the gravel path that connected the buildings. Their feet crunched the stones, and the sun heated their backs. Irwin bent his arm. "May I assist you, Miss Addams?"

She hesitated then nodded and slipped her hand into the crook of his elbow. Despite anticipating the feel of her fingers, their warmth through his shirt sleeve shot a tremor up his spine.

He licked his lips. "Uh…I need to apologize for…uh…hurting your feelings earlier when I accused you of tiring of me. You've been nothing but gracious, and my behavior…well, I'm sorry."

A smile lit her face, and she squeezed his arm. "You're forgiven. I haven't walked in your shoes, but I imagine you're going through a lot. I know how folks in Mechanicsburg treated the objectors, so I assume you've had similar experiences. It can't be easy living your convictions when the entire world seems to be against you. Then your father saddles you with a potential wife you hadn't planned on."

Irwin laid his hand over hers. "Thank you for understanding. You're a real peach."

Rochelle winked at him. "Let's start over. Right now." She pulled away from Irwin and extended her hand. "Mr. Terrell, my name is Rochelle Addams. It's nice to meet you."

He gaped at her then bowed and enveloped her hand in his. "The pleasure is all mine, Miss Addams. Would you care for a spin around the campus, then perhaps lunch in the dining hall?"

"I'd be delighted, Mr. Terrell."

His heart skipped a beat. He ran a hand through his hair then drew her hand back into his elbow. "It may not seem like it, but I have nothing against marriage. My parents were happily married for years, and I have friends who are married."

"You don't have to explain yourself."

"I'd like to."

"All right."

"See, I believe that marriage is a gift from God, not to be entered into lightly. And, well, for my father to up and call a long-lost relative to ask him if I can wed his daughter doesn't seem right. It seems rather manipulative."

"You don't think God can use humans to execute His plan? If your father's been praying about the situation, maybe he got the idea from God. Do you think that's possible?"

"Maybe. I've never had God speak to me that way."

"He deals with each of us differently, and just because He hasn't talked to you like that, doesn't mean He won't someday."

Irwin nudged her shoulder. "How'd you get to be so wise?"

She shrugged, and as expected, her face pinked. He grinned. Perhaps he'd learn to discern her thoughts after all.

"Who's Gertrude?"

Irwin reared back. "What?"

"I heard a couple of the maids talking, and they said she'd hurt you badly." She nibbled her lower lip. "They also said they didn't think I was farm material."

"Shame on them for gossiping." He patted her hand. "But you deserve to know. Gertrude is my former fiancée. She decided a week before the wedding that she loved the best man more than she loved me."

Rochelle's eyes filled with tears. "Oh, Irwin, how awful. When was that?"

"Two years ago…oh…today would be my second wedding anniversary." Hmmm. Where was the usual pain and embarrassment that accompanied thoughts of the woman who jilted him? Had he finally moved past the specter of rejection? Maybe today was about more beginnings than a just new job.

Chapter Seven

Ocean waves crashed against the shore, and seagulls swooped on the thermals in the cloudless sky. Rochelle squinted at the sunlight sparkling on the water. She and Irwin had the day off after working six days straight. He'd managed to scare up a basket and sweet-talked the cook into packing them a picnic.

Rochelle checked her watch. Still some time before she'd need to return to campus to work the night laundry shift. Her duties fluctuated. Thus far she'd served at the reception desk, in the laundry, and in the kitchen. Answering the telephone was easy, but the only time she'd had that shift, the hours crawled by. At the end of her time constantly lifting and wrestling sheets into the mangle to iron them, her shoulders ached, and her hands burned from the harsh soap, but the satisfaction of seeing a crisp, clean tower of sheets after the task was done brought a smile to her face. The vast number of meals processed in the kitchen despite rationing had seemed never-ending. She'd not had to make food deliveries to the critical ward yet, and her stomach clenched at the thought of having to do so.

She'd much rather stand behind the steel table offering food to the patients. Many shuffled past and refused to make eye contact. Others smiled and chatted, making her wonder what sort of mental illness they had.

"A seashell for your thoughts." Irwin handed her a clam shell. His crystal-blue eyes had deepened to the color of the sea, and a smile tugged at his lips.

Accepting the gift, she rubbed her fingers over the shell's ridges. "Thinking about the patients. It makes me sad they're locked up. Am I making any kind of a difference in their lives? Washing their sheets and clothes, cooking their food…" She set the shell down and began to trace its outline in the sand.

"We've only been here a week. What did you expect to happen?"

She shrugged. "I'm not sure. Not that I thought working here would be a glamorous job, but I guess I visualized myself building relationships with the patients and making them feel better, less lonely. Most of them don't have visitors. It doesn't seem right."

"You have a kind heart, Rochelle." He ran his finger across the back of her hand.

Her skin tingled where he'd touched her, and her face warmed. Why did she have to blush at the slightest provocation? He must think her silly as a school-girl. "Thank you. I wasn't fishing for a compliment."

"I didn't think you were." He collected their soiled plates and napkins and tucked them into the basket. "I know what you mean about trying to make a difference. I also want to impact their lives. As a ward attendant, I'm able to interact with the residents on a personal level, but I've got strict instructions not to discuss God unless they bring up the subject. I was hoping to pray with the men, but thus far all I've been able to do is pray for them."

"God will bless your efforts. He already has. I heard about the incident with one of the men who was having a fit. The girls were discussing the incident in the laundry room yesterday. They said you could have been injured or worse."

"That's ridiculous."

"Say what you will, and I know you've had a hard time from some of the other staff about being a CO, but they're giving you a grudging respect now. You successfully handled a patient they haven't been able to. Can you tell me what happened without breaking confidentiality?"

Irwin wiped his hands on the red-checked towel then folded the linen and laid it on top of the basket. He brushed errant crumbs from his slacks and cleared his throat. "Sure. Ned was more restless than usual the night before last. You know some of the staff call him The Tiger because of his penchant for biting and clawing during an episode. I was told to put him to bed, which as you may know is what they say when they want the patient restrained in a straitjacket."

She shuddered. "As if using the words makes it more palatable."

"Anyway, I received permission for an alternate approach. I entered his room and stood at the door and called his name. I held out my hand and asked him to hold it. Every second that ticked by felt like an eon.

My heart nearly burst out of my chest, and I thought he might attack me, but I continued to stay in position, praying he'd calm down. I don't know how much time passed, but he finally put his hand in mine."

Rochelle clapped. "That's wonderful."

"I asked him if he wanted to take a walk, and he agreed, so we came down here." He swept his arm along the shore. "We walked up and down this stretch of sand. We sat on that pile of rocks for a bit. Then in a voice barely above a whisper he said, 'Do you think I should go to bed?' We headed back to his room, and he laid down without another word. Slept through the night."

"Now who has a gentle heart, Irwin?" She giggled when his face pinked.

A harsh laugh escaped his lips. "That's the problem. Most of the staff members think I'm a sensitive coward. They've made comments that I'm afraid of combat, and I'm hiding out at the hospital. No amount of conversation about my beliefs has changed their viewpoint. Some of them have family overseas, so they resent the fact I'm here and safe. They probably wish Ned had hurt me." He rubbed his forehead and sighed.

"It's hard to be ridiculed, but God will bless you. And sometimes we're a beacon without knowing it. You said most of the staff. Are there guys who don't make fun of you?"

"Yeah, there are a few. Randolph's been nice enough. He's 4F because of a problem with his vision and has taken his share of guff for his condition. And Lester's a Christian. He's worked here for years and is too old for service. He tried to enlist, but they wouldn't take him."

"How do the others feel about those two?"

"I'm not sure. But I'm here to do a job, not necessarily make friends."

"True, but having friends helps, don't you think? Even the Bible says something about three strands not easily broken."

He chucked her under the chin. "There you go being wise again."

She shivered at his touch then searched his face. Did he feel anything, or was he simply being nice? "Thanks for suggesting the picnic. Even though we're talking about work, it has been relaxing to get away from the building. The constant noise is wearing." She picked up a handful of sand then let the grains pour from her hand. "The beach is peaceful, restful. I could sit here forever."

"Is this your first time at the ocean?"

"No. My parents took the family to Cape Cod when I was a toddler. I don't remember much about the trip other than my brother's sand castles. I would knock them down as fast as he could make them." She frowned. "I was annoying him, even back then."

"Do you not get along with Leonard?"

She studied the white caps on the water. What kind of relationship did she have with her brother? Distant memories of bike rides and playing ball filtered through her mind. "At one point, perhaps, but now…he doesn't have much use for me, and I seem to irritate him at every turn."

"His irritation is his problem, not yours."

"What do you mean?"

"Well, unless you're doing something intentionally to get on his nerves, then how he responds to your behaviors is his responsibility. Hence, his problem. The little time I've spent with you, I can't picture you being difficult."

"Clearly we haven't spent enough time together."

He snorted a laugh, and his face lit up. "Let's see if we can't remedy that."

Her heart raced. "We won't have another day off for nearly a week. What do you suggest in the meantime?"

"We could go for walks after our shift or play cards in the recreation room."

"All good ideas." She licked her lips. "Listen, I know that you're dependent on your family and church for money since you're not being paid. I could give you some of my salary if that would help."

He frowned and shook his head. "I'm doing fine financially. I can't take money from you. It wouldn't be right."

"We're supposed to be courting. You support me, and I support you."

"No. Absolutely not." His face darkened. "I won't have you giving me an allowance."

"It wouldn't be like that. Just a bit to tide you over."

"Rochelle, you've been to my home. You've seen the farm. Money is not an issue for me. Things are difficult enough here without the others finding out you're paying my way. Not another word about this. Do you understand?"

"Yes, but—"

"Not another word." He stood and grabbed the basket. "It's getting late. I need to hurry back."

Blinking away tears, she rose. She couldn't let him see how his words affected her. She'd messed up by offering him money, but did he have to react with such anger? Sure, he didn't need the cash, but she wanted to feel like part of his family, and supporting him would do that. He obviously still thought of her as an outsider. Was this courtship going to work?

Chapter Eight

Irwin finger-combed his hair as he wandered along the shoreline behind the group of patients he'd brought down for recreation. Lester, the orderly who'd been so accepting, walked beside him while Barry, one of the residents who had improved to where he could be given minor responsibilities, led his fellow patients toward an outcropping of rocks some distance away. The sun played cat and mouse with cotton-ball clouds overhead. The tide was out, leaving a wake of shells, seaweed, and tiny creatures scrabbling for cover.

From the corner of his eye he studied his coworker. Lester ambled across the sand as if he didn't have a care in the world rather than chaperoning a collection of psychiatric patients. Somewhere between fifty and seventy years old, he had the build of a middle linebacker. His scalp shone through thinning red hair. His gray eyes were bracketed by laugh lines, and despite his fair complexion his skin was tanned from spending hours outdoors with the patients.

Waves lapped gently, and a breeze brushed Irwin's face with briny fingers. Hard to believe there was a war on. Somewhere around the globe, men were shooting at each other, fighting over deep-seated ideals, both sides convinced of the righteousness of their cause. He shook his head. Why couldn't people change and move toward peaceful solutions?

Lester bumped into him. "'Tis too pretty a day for such deep thoughts. What's gotten ahold of you?" His singsong lilt conveyed his Irish roots.

"During the weeks I've been here, I've grown to love the beauty of this area." Irwin sighed. "In another time and place, I would be in a field pushing seeds into the soil, tearing out weeds, or wringing my hands over why it hadn't rained lately. Instead, I'm working in a mental hospital, with people like you."

"You were thinking about me?" Lester grinned. "Sure, and that won't get you anywhere."

Irwin chuckled. "Perhaps not, but I don't sense any sort of tension from you, and I wonder about that. We have a responsibility for these men who are unable to fend for themselves. Doesn't that worry you?"

"Nah." Lester swept his arm toward the ocean. "Most of them are too afraid to get into the water, and they don't move so fast that I can't chase them down, even at my size."

"I wish I had your confidence."

"You will. As you said, you've only been here a short while." He patted Irwin's shoulder. "It takes time to get into the swing of things. You're a farmer, yes?"

Irwin shrugged. "I was raised on a farm, but frankly, I'm not very good at it."

"The crops or the livestock?"

"I'm a complete disaster when it comes to the fields, but I love taking care of the animals."

"Excellent. Think of it like that, and you'll do just fine. Same as your cows and chickens, these poor folks are dependent on you to take care of them for their basic needs. We feed, clothe, and exercise them. The difference is that they have a soul, and no matter what their problems or state of mind, we should treat each one as a precious child of God. As we should everyone we meet. No distinction."

"You make it sound easy."

Lester held up his index finger. "Simple, yes. Easy, no. Sometimes the days are physically demanding. Others are emotionally exhausting knowing some of these people will never improve, never get better enough to be on their own. And that's sad."

"I think about that. Especially with cases like Ned. His behavior is erratic no matter what treatment they attempt."

"I leave those concerns up to the docs. Theirs is a heavy burden trying to cure their patients. We just have to care for them. And pray." Lester raised his eyebrow. "There seems more behind your introspection than worry about a new job. This wouldn't have anything to do with the lovely, young lass who came with you. I hear you're courting. I'd never be down if she was committed to marryin' me."

Irwin stuffed his hands into his pockets and kicked at the sand.

Lester grabbed his arm. "What have you done? Did you mess things up with your girl?"

"Yes. We don't see each other much because of our work schedules, but whenever we get together I manage to say the wrong things and upset her." Irwin blew out a loud breath and pulled away. "I can't think straight when I'm with her."

The Irishman guffawed. "You've got it bad."

"Got what?"

His laughter faded, but his lips continued to twitch. "Love. You're in love with her. That's why you're aiming to get married, isn't it? Good grief, lad. How'd you get this far?"

Irwin's face warmed, and he ducked his head. "Actually, my father arranged for us to wed. He decided I wasn't getting anywhere on my own, and time was wasting. Rochelle and I only met a few days before I arrived here. She seems nice, but I'm not in love with her."

Lester's eyes widened. "I didn't think you Americans set up marriages."

"We don't."

"Then why did you agree to it?"

"She'd come a long way. Father said it was a trial. It seemed only fair to give it a chance."

"But if you're not making an effort to succeed, you're not really giving it a chance, are you?"

"You don't pull any punches, Lester."

"Life's too short, lad, to go at it halfway. Now, tell me about her. All I know is she's a hard worker, and that's all well and good for an employee, but there should be more to having a wife. There needs to be excitement and wantin' to be with her because of how she makes you feel. What do you know about her?"

"You're a matchmaker in addition to being a ward attendant? I didn't realize you had so many skills."

"Someone's got to help you out. If I were a lot younger, I'd be giving you a run for your money. You going to tell me about her, or would you rather tell me how you messed up?"

Irwin held up his hands in surrender. "Okay. She's from Pennsylvania, and she has an older brother, who seems a bit overbearing if you ask me. They don't get along too well. Anyway, before she came here she was involved in the war effort with a victory garden and rolling bandages. She was also part of some sort of club that wrote letters to servicemen."

Lester rolled his eyes. "Those are just facts, lad, and I appreciate you sharin' them, but what about her. What makes her laugh? Does she have a favorite food? What's important to her? Dontcha know?"

"Rochelle has a deep faith in God. When she talks about Him, it's as if she's sitting right next to Him. She's bold in her trust of Him and is matter-of-fact when we talk about it. But in other things, she's shy and embarrasses easily. I think her brother's critical nature makes her reticent to have an opinion on anything that isn't related to her faith."

"A God-fearin' woman. That's good."

Irwin nodded. "True." His mind went back to last week's picnic and her excitement over the crabs that burrowed into the sand. He smiled. "She loves being outside. She takes delight in every aspect of creation. I've seen her enraptured with flowers and insects. She bends down to study the sea life that crawls along the beach. It's as if she's never seen them before."

"Perhaps she hasn't, or at least up close. If her brother's as heavy handed as you say, maybe she hasn't had a chance to enjoy the small things in life. Not everyone has the same opportunities, lad. You need to give her space to bloom and figure out who she is. Only then can she love another in confidence." Lester narrowed his eyes. "And you have to decide if you're going to see this through. Don't play with her emotions, Irwin. It's not fair, and she'll get hurt. She doesn't deserve that. So you've got to ask yourself if you can be the man she needs. And if you can't, you need to tell her sooner rather than later."

Irwin winced. Could he be Rochelle's husband? Did he want to be?

Chapter Nine

The buzz of women's voices blended with the cacophony of banging pots and pans, and the sound of workers' footsteps rushing back and forth inside the kitchen. Rochelle blew an errant strand of hair from her face as she kneaded the bread in front of her. Her shoulders ached, but the yeasty scent of the dough reminded her the pain would be worth it once the loaves were baked into crusty goodness. She wasn't a good cook, but she had mastered making bread. Finally, something she could do well.

"Addams, quit daydreaming. Those loaves won't make themselves."

Rochelle's face warmed at the harsh words of the kitchen matron. "Yes, ma'am."

"And if you manage to finish within the hour, get started on the carrots." The woman smirked. "See if you can do it correctly this time."

Several of the girls snickered.

Blinking back tears, Rochelle pressed down on the sticky mixture then folded the dough over itself and repeated the process until the ball was smooth under her hands. Why did the matron seem to take such pleasure at embarrassing her? The woman didn't subject any of the other workers to ridicule. Most of them kept their distance from Rochelle, as if they didn't want to be seen with her.

Dear God, help me. I feel so alone. I thought I was answering your call to serve those less fortunate, but all I've done is cook and clean, tasks I would be doing at home. Is this really where you would have me be? Surely, there is some other place I could work and still see Irwin. Then I wouldn't have to bear the derision of my coworkers.

My Son suffered mockery and death for you, My child. As his follower, do you expect better treatment than He received?

Rochelle's heart lightened. She was not alone. She'd allowed fatigue and discouragement to get the better of her. "Thank you for that reminder."

"And now you're talking to yourself? You're as loony as the patients." The matron dumped an armload of potatoes on the table. "Work faster. You'll need to scrape these as well."

"Mrs. Harridan, may I have a moment of your time somewhere private?" Her legs trembled, but Rochelle met the woman's glare with a firm look.

"You can't say what you gotta say in the kitchen?"

"I'd rather not."

"Suit yourself, but you'd better be quick about it. Time you waste talking to me is time I'll shave off your break."

Rochelle pressed her lips together and followed the stocky woman outside where they stood under a mammoth oak tree that provided blissful shade from the harsh rays of the sun.

"Mrs. Harridan, I apologize if I've offended you. Please tell me what I can do to make up for any ill will I've caused."

"What?" Confusion darkened Mrs. Harridan's face.

"You seem angry at me, and I'm sorry if I've done something to upset you. I'd like us to have a more congenial relationship. Wouldn't you?" Rochelle pinned on a smile.

"Uh…you haven't done anything wrong…well, you've made a few mistakes in the kitchen, but not everyone's cut out for cooking."

"Then why have you treated me so harshly? I'm making an effort to learn the job."

"You're a good girl. It's just that…" Her lower lip trembled, and she blew out a loud breath. She gestured to a group of men in the field. "Your fiancé. I don't understand how you can marry him. He's a conchie, hiding out here while real men go off and fight for justice against those terrible Germans and Japs."

Rochelle's shoulders stiffened. How dare this woman criticize Irwin and the other objectors. She opened her mouth to protest…

Give her My grace, child.

The air went out of Rochelle's lungs, and she hung her head. Once again, she'd almost let her temper get in the way. Fortunately, God's small voice prevented her from responding in anger. She licked her lips and wiped her damp palms on her apron. "Do you have someone special in the service, Mrs. Harridan? Is that why you don't like the objectors?"

"Two of my sons." She sniffled. "And I haven't heard from either one in four months. I don't know where they are or if they're even still…alive."

"How awful. I'm sorry for your distress, but…ah…the men who choose not to carry weapons aren't hiding. They feel strongly about their convictions not to go into combat. Irwin is a Christian, and he feels the Bible tells him not to join the military."

Mrs. Harridan frowned. "Then does he think what my son and the other soldiers, sailors, and airmen are doing is wrong? He shouldn't judge them."

"He's not. He feels each man must make the decision that's right for him." Rochelle cocked her head. "If you don't like the objectors, why did you sign the release saying you were okay with them working here?"

"I didn't feel like I had a choice. The higher-ups made a big deal about how we were helping the government and ourselves since we've been so shorthanded since the war began. Lots of men and women joined up or got drafted. We don't pay as much as the manufacturing plants, so it's been difficult to find people to take our jobs." She lowered her eyes. "I'm sorry I've treated you badly. I just don't know what to do with all this anger I got inside me."

Rochelle's stomach fluttered as if Fred Astaire was tap dancing inside her belly. What should she say to this poor woman?

Mrs. Harridan turned toward the kitchen. "Anyway, I'll try to be nice from now on, but I can't promise anything about your fiancé. It hurts to think of him here and my boys in danger somewhere out there."

"I understand, because I struggled with getting mad. It made me say and do things I shouldn't. In fact, sometimes I still mess up, but I became a Christian, and now I have help from God and His Son Jesus to be a better person. Would you…uh…like to hear about that?"

"Maybe later. I gotta check on the roast that is still in the oven for lunch and then take inventory so I can make my order. It's getting harder and harder to create meals out of what's available. I'll be glad when the gardens start producing." Her mouth curved into a timid smile. "And you've gotta finish the bread and vegetables."

Rochelle executed a mock salute and grinned. "Yes, ma'am. I'm glad we're going to be friends, and I'll be praying for your boys, that they are safe, and you hear from them soon."

"You'd do that for me after how I treated you?"

"That's all in the past, but I'm supposed to care about you even if we weren't getting along. Thanks for taking time to speak with me. You didn't have to. You could have ignored my request."

"Like I said, Miss Addams, you're a good girl." She jerked her head toward the men across the yard. "Let the orderlies know we're a bit behind schedule. Say about thirty minutes. The extra dose of sunshine should prove beneficial. Your man is over there, but don't dawdle."

"Okay." Rochelle wrapped Mrs. Harridan in a quick hug.

"Now, we'll have none of that." Her pink face and pleased expression belied her words.

With a chuckle, Rochelle hurried across the lush grass. Irwin and Lester looked up, and she waved. Lester returned her greeting, but Irwin's face remained impassive. Was he not happy to see her? They'd made some progress in getting to know each other, but he still held back.

Should she tell him about the incident with Mrs. Harridan? Would he care? Perhaps as a fellow Christian, but it might bother him to know the woman disliked him because of his convictions. He was already the target of derision from other staff. If only they could accept his faith. He'd proven himself with the patients.

She drew alongside Lester and passed the message about lunch.

Irwin scowled. "It's important the men remain on schedule. Why are you girls late providing lunch?"

"I apologize for the inconvenience, but it couldn't be helped." Rochelle narrowed her eyes. "I'll see you gentlemen in the dining hall." She pivoted on her heel and marched toward the kitchen. Could she marry a man who was moodier than a toddler? Would Irwin ever love her?

Chapter Ten

Irwin tugged at a stubborn clump of grass that had infiltrated one of the victory gardens behind the kitchen. The chunk broke free, and dirt shot into the air, spattering Irwin. Grimacing, he spat out the grit then used his handkerchief to wipe the soil from his face. He climbed to his feet, stumbled to the pump, and worked the handle up and down, listening to the gurgle head to the surface.

The muscles in his arm contracted as he gripped the rusted iron pipe. Water spewed from the faucet, and he ducked his head under the frigid flow, rubbing the soil and debris from his hair and skin. The stream beat a tempo on the ground, creating a muddy patch around the pump. The scent of his sweat mingled with the smell of the sodden grass.

Getting as clean as possible from washing in the spray, he grabbed one of the towels draped on a nearby chair and dried himself. He returned to the garden and glanced at his three charges. The men knelt around the edge of the garden plot and stabbed at the ground with their trowels. Rather than concentration, their expressions held vacant stares.

Expelling a deep sigh, Irwin strode to their location. "How's it going, gents? A nice day to be outside, isn't it?"

Two of the residents flinched when he spoke, while the other continued to poke at the dirt.

"Like this, Jesse." Irwin shoved his trowel deep into the ground on one side of a broad-leafed weed. He repeated the motion until he'd circled the plant and the roots had loosened their hold on the earth. With his free hand, he pulled out the plant. "See? Now, you try it."

Mute, Jesse nodded and mimicked Irwin's motions, but his efforts only removed a portion of the weed. His face lit up, and he grinned.

Irwin winced.

Jesse's smile faltered. "Not right, Irwin?"

"You did great, Jesse. Keep up the good work." Irwin patted the man's shoulder. "Are you thirsty? I could bring you a cup of water."

The man shrugged. "Maybe later, when I finish."

"Okay, but don't get overheated. I'll be back to check on you in a while." Irwin rose and made his way to the other patients. Hopefully, he wouldn't discourage them like he'd obviously done with Jesse. The man had seen Irwin's disappointment and been hurt by his reaction. Why did he think he could work with the mentally ill? Despite the training, he continued to make mistakes with the residents. He massaged his forehead in a futile attempt to remove the memory of past errors.

Maybe he should have volunteered for one of the experiments the government was conducting at a select group of the country's medical schools. Would he be brave enough to get injected with hepatitis or malaria? Or an unknown disease? He shuddered.

One of the COs had a brother in Minnesota who was part of a starvation experiment. Irwin rubbed his stomach. The residents and staff ate well at Shady Hills. Could he go without eating for days at a time? Perhaps the employees who called him yellow-bellied were right.

Irwin closed his eyes. *Dear God, I'm at a loss here. I keep messing up my job. These people deserve an attendant who won't put their lives at risk. I don't mean to question You, but am I in the right place? Did I hear*

Your call correctly for me to serve at a mental hospital? Rochelle seems
so sure of herself, and she's done better than I have at ministering here.
Help me be a better employee…a better man.

"You okay, Irwin?"

His eyelids flew open.

Jesse stood in front of him holding a cup of water, concern etched
on his face. "You need a drink?"

"Thank you." *And thank You, Father.* "Just what I needed, Jesse.
How did you know?"

"You looked thirsty."

Irwin clapped him on the back then beckoned to the pair of
residents still working in the garden. He could learn a lot from Jesse. "I
think we should take a break. You've worked hard and should rest."

The men left their garden tools and followed him to the water
station where they drank their fill then walked to a pair of wooden benches
nestled under one of the campus's mammoth beech trees. In the distance,
the clock on the administration building chimed thrice. Irwin checked his
watch. It had the correct time.

A giggle sounded, and his head whipped around to find the source. His eyes darted back and forth. Where did the laughter originate? Deep chuckling came from behind a stand of bushes, and he squinted at the tangle of branches. Should he investigate?

"Ah, luv, yer killing me. That's a wonderful story."

Irwin recognized Lester's brogue, and he crept closer.

"You're just saying that." Rochelle's warm, contralto voice held a note of amusement.

Irwin froze. A burning sensation rose in his chest, and he clenched his teeth. How dare Lester hide away to meet with Rochelle out of sight from others. Did he care nothing for her reputation?

"No, lass, you have a sparkling sense of humor, although you shouldn't poke fun at yourself, even in jest. We're all God's creatures, and as such, have value, no matter how foolish our behaviors."

"You're right, Lester, but there's a reason the Bible refers to us as sheep. Sometimes we're not much smarter than those poor animals. That's why I enjoy working with them down in the barn. They remind me of my need for God and His guiding hand."

"I prefer the animals to working in the fields. 'Tis not near so backbreaking, and the beasts are grateful for everything I do. The plants don't seem to show any gratitude, dontcha know?"

Rochelle and Lester snickered, their voices blending in harmony.

Irwin's stomach tightened. Their conversation was innocent, yet tentacles of jealousy ensnared him. Did Rochelle care for Lester? He had thirty years or more on her, but love was no respecter of age. Who knew why some people fell in love and others did not?

He pressed his lips together. What if she chose Lester over him? His breath hitched. He'd survive, like he'd done when Gertrude jilted him, but it would be a painful journey to acceptance. Somewhere along the way, he'd fallen in love with Rochelle. Her sweet nature and unwavering faith had burrowed their way into his heart—his bruised, frightened heart.

His shoulders slumped. But she didn't know how he felt. No wonder she was drawn to Lester. Irwin straightened. He'd treated their relationship like a business arrangement. Yes, he'd been gracious and polite, but that wasn't enough. He had to show her how special she was. Words wouldn't be enough. His behavior needed to change.

They both had tomorrow off. He would make it a day she wouldn't forget, and with any luck she'd agree to marry him…because she wanted to, not as a way to get away from her family or because she thought she had no choice.

He peered through the branches.

Rochelle leaned toward Lester, one hand on his chest. She kissed his cheek then bent and retrieved a large square basket filled with towels. She spun on her heel and walked toward the brick building that housed the laundry facilities.

Irwin wilted. She did care for the older man.

Lester watched her leave then turned toward Irwin. "How much longer you gonna stand there gawkin'?"

Irwin reared back and rushed around the bushes. "You knew I was there? Why didn't you say anything?"

"You seemed content to be spying on us." Lester shook his head. "Are you ever gonna admit your feelings for the lass?"

"That was my plan until she kissed you. Have you been seeing her behind my back? I thought you had more honor than that."

Lester's face darkened. "I'll thank you not to question my integrity, lad. That's jealousy talkin', so I'll overlook your words. But have a care, lad, and don't do it again."

"I know what I saw."

"And appearances can be deceiving." Lester jabbed Irwin's chest with his finger. "Don't go jumpin' to conclusions. I'm not stealin' your lass. I happened to pass while she was taking down the wash, and she looked discouraged. I did my best to cheer her up, and apparently she's grateful. Nothing more. It's you she loves, and if you weren't so caught up in yourself, you'd know it. Now, get out of your own way, and show her what she means to you. She won't wait forever, and the next man might not be as accommodating as I am."

Chapter Eleven

Rochelle held out her hand to the chestnut-colored quarter horse and tried not to tremble. Puffs of hot breath tickled her skin as the animal sniffed her then touched her with its velvety-soft nose. She'd agreed to go riding with Irwin, but now that she was close to the mammoth beast, the venture didn't seem like a good idea. What if she fell off? What if she got trampled? What if she made a fool of herself?

"Relax." Irwin stroked her shoulder causing her to tremble for a different reason. "That's just Molly's way of giving you a handshake. I think she likes you. We'll stay in the corral until you're comfortable, then we can hit the trail."

She closed her eyes and nodded. His calm assurance combined with the spicy scent of his aftershave caused her pulse to skitter, but she couldn't let him know how he affected her. Theirs was strictly a business relationship. If only her heart remembered that fact.

"Now, let me show you how to check the tack to ensure it's safe. The stable boy should have done so, but as the rider, it's incumbent upon you to look as well." He ran his hands along the straps, bending and inspecting the leather. "No cracks. Good." Then, jiggling the hardware, he pointed to where the pieces were attached. "You want to look for signs of wear or rust to make sure nothing will break."

"That makes sense. Father inspects his car before he gets in to drive."

"Exactly." He grinned. "See? You know more than you think. Riding a horse is no different, but if the equipment fails the animal could get injured. We don't want that."

"No, that would be terrible."

Irwin gestured to the beltlike piece buckled around the horse's belly. "This is the girth, and it keeps the saddle in place. You don't want it too tight or too loose. Look for burrs, wads of hair, or other debris that might cause irritation to the horse." He patted Molly's nose. "You ready for a ride, girl?"

The horse whinnied and bobbed her head as if to say "yes."

Rochelle's eyes widened. "I didn't know she could talk."

A chuckle rumbled in his chest. "Molly's a smart one. She's trained for riding, but when her owner got drafted, his wife gave her and Blackie to Shady Hills. Because of gas rationing, the hospital decided to retrain the two of them for the plow. Dr. O'Dwyer has also started using the pair with a few of the patients. Horses can sense emotions long before humans can identify the feelings. The doctor thinks time spent with the animals will be good for the residents." Irwin gestured toward Molly. "Now, let's get you in the saddle."

Sweat broke out along Rochelle's hairline. She licked her lips and eyed the stirrup. Could she do this? *Lord, keep me safe!*

"I won't let anything happen to you. Just follow my lead, and you'll be fine."

"Okay." She rubbed her moist palms on the slacks Irwin had pulled out of the donation pile. Ill-fitting in the waist and too long in the leg, they hung on her like laundry on a clothesline. The denim shirt was a size too big and flapped in the breeze. She must look like a scarecrow.

She wrapped the reins around her hands, put the other hand on the saddle, and then stuck her oxford-shod foot into the stirrup. "Here I go." She hopped on her left foot a couple of times, then heaved her right leg over the horse and dropped into the saddle.

Molly shook her mane and side-stepped. She rolled her eyes back toward Rochelle.

"Sorry, Molly." Rochelle's face scorched, and she patted the animal's neck, its coarse hair rough under her hand. The horse could feel her nerves, just like Irwin had said. Molly could probably hear Rochelle's pounding heart, too.

Irwin tapped Rochelle's fingers that held the leather straps in a death grip. "Ease up. You want to lead her, not be a dictator. Think about holding the reins like you're carrying an ice cream cone: not so snug as to break it but firm enough not to drop the ice cream. And try not to press too tightly with your knees. Many beginners clamp onto the poor beasts like a clothes pin."

A nervous titter escaped Rochelle's lips. "Don't say clothespin. I've washed so many sheets in the last week, I don't want to think about doing the wash until tomorrow."

"I promise not to say another word on the topic." He executed a mock salute. "The only other thing you need to know at this point is not to yank on the reins to steer the horse. To direct her, move the rein in the direction you want to go in a motion like opening a door. If you want to stop, pull down on the reins and lean back just a bit. You want to give cues to your horse, not demands."

Rochelle swallowed against the lump in her throat. She could do this. She would do this.

He mounted the sleek black horse standing nearby, in one fluid motion. "And Rochelle…"

"Yes?" She tilted her head.

"Don't forget to breathe."

Her breath exploded in a gasp.

He threw his head back and guffawed.

Torn between embarrassment and amusement, Rochelle sighed then gave in to laughter.

Still smiling, Irwin said, "Okay, we'll walk side by side in a circle for a while then we'll turn in the other direction. I'll be here the whole time."

Rochelle adjusted her hold on the reins, then applied pressure to Molly's sides with her thighs, and the horse moved forward at a steady pace. "Oh, look! We're walking."

Irwin grinned. "Yes, you are. Good girl, Molly."

"Hey. What about me?" Rochelle pursed her lips into a pout.

"You're doing swell. Keep going. One circuit around the ring isn't enough to call you trail ready."

"Don't I know it." For the next twenty minutes, Rochelle circled the corral in clockwise then in the counter clockwise direction. Molly's rocking motion soothed her, and her limbs loosened. Her breathing slowed. She might not make a fool of herself after all.

Irwin clapped silently then motioned for her to stop. His eyes sparkled above his wide smile.

She realized she was grinning like Carroll's Cheshire Cat and covered her mouth.

"You're doing well, city girl. Do you want to try walking around the barn?"

Her pulse skipped then settled. He promised not to let anything happen to her. She had to start trusting him at some point. She shrugged and swept her arm toward the gate before taking a rein in each hand. "Let's hit the trail. After you, sir."

A smile still lighting up his face, Irwin winked at her and guided his horse to line up beside hers. "The path is wide enough for us to ride together. That way we can converse if you'd like."

"All right. Let's go, Molly." The mare's warmth permeated Rochelle's pants. Her mind raced. Sit up straight. Don't squeeze the horse. Don't clench the reins. Keep your feet in the stirrups. Perspiration trickled between her shoulder blades. She'd done fine in the corral. Why was she suddenly terrified?

"If you don't wish to discuss laundry, what would you like to talk about?"

"Hmmm?"

"I thought if we chatted, you might be less concerned about riding. Molly knows what she's doing, and she'll most likely follow Blackie."

"So I can concentrate on not falling off."

"Something like that."

"She does seem sweet."

"What's it to be? Books? Last night's episode of *The Billie Burke Show*? Or how about *The Falcon*?"

"I love *The Falcon*, but the girls wanted to listen to Jimmy Durante and dance. Frankly, I don't know how they had the energy after working a ten-hour shift, but they pulled it off. Watching Elsie and Naomi jitterbug most of the night tired me out."

"Don't you like to dance?"

"Yes, but I haven't done much. Father didn't often grant permission for me to attend the community parties and bond rallies. When I did go, Leonard stood close to me and scowled. Needless to say, his presence discouraged most of boys."

"We'll have to remedy your lack of dancing experience on our next day off. Would you like that?"

"I would."

The horses' hooves beat a steady clip-clop on the ground, and Rochelle gradually synced her body's motion with Molly's. Her ears twitched, and her head bobbed as she plodded along the trail. A gust of wind ruffled the mare's mane. The lemony scent of sweetbay magnolia mingled with Molly's musky smell, and Rochelle searched the landscape for the white blossoms nestled in glistening dark green leaves. A short distance away, the branches of a thirty-foot tree undulated in the breeze. It was easy to forget the country was at war.

Time passed while they rode in silence.

Rochelle glanced at Irwin. The brim of his fedora cast a shadow over his face, so she couldn't read his expression. Then he turned to her, and the sun lit up his eyes like blue flames. Squinting against the glare, he smiled.

Her breath caught. Did he have any idea how handsome he was?

Above their heads, a squirrel scolded them, and a pair of waxwings called to each other among the trees. Foliage rustled, and the chatter of chipmunks punctuated the air.

"Do—"

"I—"

They laughed, and Rochelle cleared her throat. "Go ahead."

"No, ladies first."

Molly nickered then arched her neck and flattened her ears.

Irwin reached over and rubbed the mare's head. "Something on your mind, girl?"

Rochelle sighed. He was gentle and kind, unselfish, and full of integrity. Could she make him love her? Was it fair to expect him to propose marriage if he had no romantic feelings for her?

"Rochelle, what are you thinking?"

She nibbled the inside of her lip and blinked away the tears that threatened to fall. "Thank you for spending your day off with me. I enjoy our time together. You're smart, funny, and gracious. I wish I could be what you need. I can't cook, I've never done farm work, and the animals scare me. You deserve someone better than me."

His eyebrows shot up, and his face darkened. "Don't—"

With a loud squawk, a crow swooped from the sky and landed next to Molly.

The horse whinnied and pranced, her front feet tapping a staccato beat on the hard-packed earth.

Rochelle cried out and clenched her knees.

Molly shot forward, and Rochelle grabbed the saddle horn with one hand while holding the reins in the other. "Molly, stop! Stop!"

The horse continued to gallop.

Rochelle bounced in the seat, her body jerking back and forth. Wind tugged at the pins in her hair, and her eyes teared. *Dear God, save me!*

———————◆———————

Irwin's heart pounded, and a chill swept over him. Rochelle clung to Molly's back like a tick on a hound dog, her screams piercing the forest. *Please, Lord, don't let her fall off. Help me catch her.*

He slapped the reins and tightened his knees. Blackie sprang forward. Irwin hunched over the horse. He felt like a jockey approaching the finish line. The gelding's mane blew in the breeze and slapped at Irwin's face. His hat flew off.

"Faster, Blackie. We've got to save our girls."

Blackie's ears pricked up, and he surged ahead. His hooves thundered on the ground, his sides heaving in exertion.

"Good boy."

They drew nearer to Molly who stumbled, then slowed.

"Hang on, Rochelle. I'm coming."

At the sound of his voice, she turned. Tears streaked her white face. Her golden-brown eyes were wide with terror, and her hair was a tangled mass. His heart skipped a beat. He had to save her.

Leaning close to Blackie's ear, he said, "H'ya, Blackie. We must be closer. You can do it. You're a strong boy."

The horse's muscles bunched as he strained to pick up speed. He came alongside Molly, and she glanced toward her brother. Her eyes wide, the whites were fully visible around her pupils. She snorted and pulled against the reins.

Irwin gave Blackie his head so the horse could keep pace with his sister. Winded, she began to slow, and a few minutes later she stopped, her head drooping in fatigue. Her sides contracted and expanded, her breathing ragged.

Sobbing, Rochelle released the reins and slid off the horse, falling to the ground in a heap.

Irwin launched himself from the saddle and rushed to her side. He gathered her in his lap. With one hand, he brushed the hair from her face and rubbed her back with the other. Her body quavered and shook. She clung to him and cried.

After several moments, her tears stopped, and she sniffled. Pushing away from him, she wiped at the wetness on her cheek with her sleeve. She took a deep shuddering breath. "Thank you for saving me. I didn't know what to do. My fright was feeding Molly's fear. Please don't be mad at her."

He stroked her cheek. "Always thinking of others, aren't you, love?"

At the endearment, she gasped then stilled in his arms. "You've never…"

"I know, and I hope you'll forgive me."

She froze in his embrace, uncertainty lining her face. She dropped her gaze.

He rubbed her back, and she stiffened. "This isn't the way I wanted it to happen. I came out here today with the notion of a romantic horseback ride at the end of which I'd ask you to marry me. I've made a mess of our agreement. Lester warned me I was going to lose you, and I almost did."

Her head shot up. "You talked about me with Lester? Why would you do that?"

His breathing hitched. "I saw you yesterday with him at the clothesline. I…uh…made an assumption about the two of you. I thought you cared for him…You kissed his cheek…He set me straight, and our conversation made me realize I was scared to let you in. Gertrude did a number on me, and I let that color how I treated you, but I love you. I know that now. My life is so much better with you in it. I—"

She giggled and pressed her fingers to his lips. "Yes."

"Yes?"

"I love you, too, and, yes, I'll marry you."

He pulled her to him in a tight embrace then released her and kissed her forehead. "Is our next day off too soon?"

Chapter Twelve

Mrs. Harridan banged out Bach's *Jesu, Joy of Man's Desiring* on the out-of-tune piano in the hospital's cavernous gymnasium that doubled as a chapel on Sundays. Periodic wrong notes peppered her rendition, and Irwin winced. After the kitchen matron heard about Rochelle's engagement to him, the woman insisted she be allowed to play for the wedding. It'd seemed like a generous offer at the time. Not exactly the experience he wanted for Rochelle.

Surrounded by vases of sweet-smelling wildflowers, he pressed his hand against his middle to quell the rising nausea, and Father, who'd agreed to be his best man, patted his shoulder. Once he received the telephone call about the wedding, he and Earnest sprang into action. They'd managed to secure a dress for Rochelle, food for the guests, and an extra ration of gasoline for the two-night honeymoon. Whirlwind didn't describe the speed at which things came together for the event.

The door opened in the back of the room, and his breath caught. Rochelle hesitated in the doorway, a shimmering pool of sunshine casting a glow around her. A white pillbox hat with a small veil covering her face perched on her glossy hair. The knee-length, white dress had a frothy, lace skirt with a simple, scoop-neck bodice. A strand of pearls lay at her neck, and she wore white pumps. How Father had come up with a dress that fit perfectly was nothing short of a miracle, and she'd never looked more beautiful. Irwin smiled. Of course, she was pretty no matter what her outfit.

Lord, thank You for Rochelle. Help me be a good husband to her.

In one hand, Rochelle held a bouquet of pink and white roses, and her other was tucked into her father's elbow as she glided down the aisle toward the front of the room, her eyes shadowed by the netting. Was she also nervous?

Mrs. Harridan hit a clinker with gusto, then her fingers slid onto the correct note and held it until Rochelle arrived at Irwin's side. Dimples framed her mouth, and she glanced at him, rolling her eyes as she gave an imperceptible nod toward the pianist. He should have known she would find amusement in the situation rather than disappointment at the lack of perfection. Did her grace know no bounds? He hoped so because he would surely need it during their marriage.

Reverend Wyncoop, Rochelle's pastor who'd driven to Delaware to officiate, gestured for the guests to be seated then looked at Rochelle's father. "Who gives this woman to be wed?"

"Her mother and I do." Mr. Addams's quiet voice was firm. He took Rochelle's hand and laid it on Irwin's then lifted her veil to kiss her cheek. He whispered something in her ear, and she returned his kiss with a sigh then said something in return. Irwin's heart tugged at the sight of their precious exchange.

Mr. Addams stepped away and sat on the front pew next to his wife and son, whose expression wasn't quite a grimace. Did he object to Irwin or to Rochelle's marriage in general?

"Dearly beloved, we are gathered here to join these two young people in holy matrimony, and I'm sure you're anxious to see them wed, but first I'd like to share a few words to the couple." He leaned close to Irwin and Rochelle. "Don't worry. This won't take long."

Rochelle giggled, and Irwin glanced at her and grinned. With only a few words, the minister had calmed his nerves.

"Marriage is a partnership, and whether we mean to or not, we often think of a partnership as involving two parties. But that's not the case here. Irwin and Rochelle are Christians which means that God is the third member of their partnership, and to take the analogy a bit further, He's the senior partner, much like in a law firm where there is one leader to set the vision of the organization. Irwin's job as the husband is to follow God's leading, and Rochelle is to honor and obey that leadership."

He looked over his glasses at the congregation. "Now, men, before you get self-satisfied thinking that you're in charge, and your wife needs to trail behind you in blind acquiescence, consider what the Bible says about husbands. Paul tells us in Ephesians that we are to love our wives as Christ loved the church, giving Himself up for her. In other words dying for her. We are to put our wives' needs above our own and be willing to lay down our lives for them. Suddenly it doesn't seem so easy now, does it?"

A murmur rustled through the guests.

"Before you get discouraged, men, remember that God is with you every step of the way. He will give you strength for the journey if you listen. In the good times and the bad."

Irwin squeezed Rochelle's hand. He would commit the pastor's wise words to memory.

After addressing the women's role in the marriage, Reverend Wyncoop winked at Irwin and Rochelle. "Now, to the part of the ceremony you've been waiting for. Perhaps patiently. Perhaps not."

The crowd laughed, and Irwin chuckled. He glanced at Rochelle whose face glowed with a healthy pink. He would never tire of looking at this lovely woman.

Pastor Wynkoop guided them through their vows, and moments later the ceremony ended.

Irwin grasped Rochelle's hand, and they paraded down the aisle while the guests applauded. His heart swelled. *Thank you, God, for making all of this work out. Please bless our union as only You can.*

A cloth-covered table stood in the back of the room and held a three-tiered cake. Platters of sandwiches and sweets surrounded the chocolate-frosted confection. Father must have called in a lot of favors to secure the amount of sugar required for the spread.

He squeezed Rochelle's fingers as they approached the table. The guests clustered nearby watching as she picked up the gleaming knife. He laid his hand on hers, and they cut the fragrant cake. They each picked up a piece.

Irwin wiggled his eyebrows and motioned that he planned to smear the delicacy on her nose.

Rochelle giggled. "Don't you dare."

He gave her a quick kiss, and then they fed each other a bite of cake, while their friends, family, and coworkers oohed and aahed. Even the colleagues who'd denigrated him in the beginning seemed to be celebrating with him. Or perhaps it was simply the opportunity to enjoy foods not typically available.

"A seashell for your thoughts." Rochelle tilted her head, her eyebrows drawn together. "Are you okay? You're supposed to be happy. It's our wedding day."

"You know me too well. I was ruminating over the fact that some of the men who have been…er…difficult are here looking happy for me. I was trying to determine why."

She patted his arm. "Everyone loves a wedding, even for people they don't care for. But maybe today has broken down some of the barriers. They see you are just like them." She nudged his shoulder. "Now, let's grab a plate. I'm famished. I couldn't eat earlier."

"Too nervous?"

She flushed and nodded.

"Me too. I'd much rather have eloped, but I wanted you to have the wedding of your dreams."

"Thanks, Irwin. That means a lot to me."

Earl, one of the more troublesome orderlies, walked toward them. Irwin's stomach clenched. Would they ruin his big day?

Irwin lifted his hand in greeting. "Hello, Earl. Thanks for coming. Please make sure you get something to eat."

Earl looked at Rochelle. "Seems mighty fast for you two getting married. Everything all right?"

"What are you insinuating, Earl?"

The man shoved his hands into his front pockets and rocked on his heels. "I was kind of surprised when I got the invitation. You two have only been here a few weeks, and now you're getting married. Did you have to?"

Irwin ground his teeth, and his muscles tensed. "Why you—"

Rochelle stroked Irwin's arm then smiled at Earl. "Thank you for celebrating with us. Irwin and I knew each other before arriving at Shady Hills, and we didn't want to wait any longer to be married. Our relationship and marriage has been a miracle from God. May I tell you about it?"

"Well, uh…"

"Excellent. I'm glad you asked." She proceeded to share the story of how Mr. Terrell brought her to his home and their subsequent agreement to explore a possible marriage.

Irwin swallowed a grin at the expression of wonder on Earl's face. Rochelle had the man enthralled with her words, and Irwin would have ruined the opportunity by arguing. He was going to learn so much from her.

"Isn't it exciting how God worked this all out?" She laid her hand on Earl's arm. "He took a personal interest in our lives. Otherwise, we'd never have met and fallen in love. And now look at us. We're so blessed. Has God worked anything like that for you?"

"He and I aren't on speaking terms."

"I'm sorry to hear that. A similar thing happened to me. I was angry at God for perceived injustices, and I turned my back on Him. Fortunately, I realized how wrong I was, and now I can't imagine my life without Him. You could have that relationship, too, Earl. I'd be happy to tell you how."

Earl backed up and waved his hands. "Another time, miss…I mean Mrs. Terrell. This is your wedding day. You shouldn't spend it talking to a scalawag like me."

"You're no more a scalawag than I am, Earl."

"No, ma'am. You're an angel."

"That's sweet of you to say, but we all need God, even me. Would you like Irwin to share with you how you can have a relationship with Him?"

Eyes wide, Earl glanced at Irwin then shook his head. "Listen, I know I've not been real nice to you since you came. I had a hard time agreeing with your politics, but I've been watching you, and I see you're true to your word, your convictions. I still don't agree with them, but I don't think you're a coward. You're a stand-up guy." He ducked his head. "I'm sorry about being mean and riling up the others against you."

Irwin tried not to gape at the man, whose normal behavior included jibes, insults, and profanity. "Thanks for saying that, Earl. It means a lot. Let's put everything behind us and start over."

Irwin extended his hand.

Earl shook it then bowed. "I won't take any more of your time. Enjoy your honeymoon, and I'll talk to you when you get back."

"Are you sure you can't stay? I could explain everything."

"Nah, the padre's been bugging me to attend services. Maybe I'll show up tomorrow." He chuckled. "Can't wait to see his face when I darken the doorway." With a wave, he sauntered toward a group of his cronies.

Irwin wrapped his arms around Rochelle in a strong embrace. "You, my lovely bride, are an amazing woman. I would have never guessed in a month of Sundays I'd be witnessing to a belligerent coworker at my wedding reception. What other adventures are in store for us?"

July 1944, one year later

Chapter Thirteen

A hot breeze ruffled the gauzy curtain in the so-called kitchen of the tiny apartment, and Rochelle dabbed at the perspiration on her face. Two burners, miniscule oven, and a sink too small to wash a platter hardly qualified, but it was better than the facilities in the dormitories where the single staff lived.

She circled the three-room lodging, running a cloth over the few sticks of furniture to rid the tops of the ever-present dust. Her first day off in two weeks, and she was stuck in the house cleaning. So much for celebrating her one-year anniversary. But at least she was home. A glance at the ornate, wood-and-brass mantle clock they'd received from Irwin's family as a wedding present told her he wouldn't be home from work for another six hours.

Her stomach rumbled. She dropped the towel on the counter then opened the pantry and rummaged inside. Two apples, a hunk of bread, and a misshapen lump of cheese. She sniffed the tangy, waxed-paper-wrapped chunk, and her mouth watered. A gift from Irwin's church along with a collection of canned goods, the fragrant slab had lasted nearly three weeks despite the heat. Good thing since neither she nor Irwin had the time nor the energy to shop with the few coupons and coins remaining in the cookie tin.

A knock sounded at the door. She returned the cheese to the pantry then patted her kerchief-covered head. Who was visiting in the middle of a weekday? Her heart clenched. Had something happened at the hospital?

She rushed to the door and yanked it open.

Claire stood in the hallway, a self-satisfied grin on her face and an overflowing hamper in her arms.

"Claire!" Rochelle pressed a hand on her chest where her thundering heart surely could be heard by her best friend. "What on earth are you doing here? How—"

"This basket weighs a ton. Let me in, and I'll give you the skinny."

Rochelle stepped back and swung the door wider. "I can't believe it's you."

Claire staggered into the apartment, her gaze flitting around the cramped quarters, one eyebrow raised. "Not exactly the Ritz, but it'll do." She set the basket on the café table where Irwin and Rochelle took their meals then grabbed Rochelle in a bear hug, enveloping her in the powdery scent of Ivory soap.

Tears sprang to Rochelle's eyes, and she blinked them away. *Thank you, God, for sending Claire. You knew exactly what I needed.*

"You're squeezing the life out of me, Rochelle. You've mistaken me for that good-looking husband of yours."

Rochelle released her, and a shaky giggle escaped. "Not in that outfit, I don't."

Claire curtsied then twirled, the navy polka-dot skirt swishing and dancing with her movements. Her white cotton blouse sported a lace collar, and a glistening string of pearls lay at the base of her throat.

"How can you look so pressed and fresh in this weather? I'm more wilted than a daisy after a drought."

"You always were more bothered by the heat than I am, but in all honesty, I stopped off at the hostel to wash up before coming over. I was a tad travel weary when I arrived."

"Couldn't you get a regular hotel room?"

"Didn't try. The rate was right, and it's close enough for me to walk to your place. Why waste time riding the bus back and forth?" She poked out her lower lip and huffed a breath that blew the errant strands of hair from her face. "I'm starving. Let's dig in while we catch up. Any danger of getting a glass of iced tea? And how about some tunes?"

Rochelle grinned. Claire hadn't changed a bit. Sweeping into a room like she owned it, knowing exactly what she wanted. "I'll get the tea, and you can turn on the radio. Reception isn't too good, but we do get a couple of stations."

"Swell." Claire fiddled with the knob, and static-filled music crackled and popped.

Glasses clinked as Rochelle pulled them from the cabinet and set them on the counter. She withdrew a pitcher of tea from the icebox and filled the cups with amber liquid. "I'm afraid it's unsweetened. We've been working too many hours to shop, and the last time I was at the grocer he was out of sugar."

Claire wrinkled her nose. "It hasn't been easy to find sugar at home either, so Mother has been purchasing honey from one of the neighbors who starting beekeeping last year."

They seated themselves at the table, and Claire wrenched the red-and-white-checked towel from the basket with a flourish. "Voilà! The church ladies outdid themselves with this care package. There are a ton of canned goods, plus two loaves of freshly baked bread, and a quart of cherries."

Rochelle's eyes widened. "Cherries? That's fantastic. I can make Irwin's favorite pie." Her lips trembled. "Well, at least I can try."

"Hey, what gives?" Claire grabbed Rochelle's hands and peered into her face.

"I'm a total failure." Her eyes welled, and tears rolled down her cheeks. "At home anyway. I'm doing all right at Shady Hills because I'm assigned to the laundry room for the most part and work as a ward attendant two days a week. I haven't messed up with those jobs yet."

"Things can't be that bad, can they?"

Rochelle shrugged. "I'm still not very good at cooking. I've gotten tips from Mrs. Harridan, but the meals never come out right. The meat is too dry or the vegetables overcooked. I even managed to burn the potatoes last week. I borrowed a Grace Livingston Hill book from the hospital library and was so caught up in reading that I didn't pay attention to dinner. All the water boiled out of the pot. The potatoes were so scorched they stuck to the bottom. Irwin said he didn't mind, but they were awful. And with all the rationing, it wasn't like I could throw them out in good conscience."

"It takes time to learn new skills. You'll get better."

"Today is our wedding anniversary, Claire. I've…wait a minute…is that why you're here?"

"Yes, ma'am. I couldn't make it to the wedding, so the least I could do was bring you treats for your anniversary. That, and I've got an interview tomorrow."

"At Shady Hills?"

Claire nodded. "I've missed you. Mechanicsburg isn't the same without you, and typing up reports at the naval depot might be important, but it's boring as all get-out. So I quit."

"And they let you?"

"Yeah, they were none too happy, but there wasn't anything they could do about it. It's not like my employment was mandated."

Rochelle shook her head. "But you don't have a new job yet."

"I'm doing okay. I'm still at home with Mother and Daddy, so my expenses are minimal. I help out with the groceries and some of the other bills, but I have a little money set aside." She squeezed Rochelle's fingers. "Anyway, enough about me. What else is going on? It's not like you to fall apart about a little cooking mishap."

"It's more than that—"

"Okay, fine, but you know what I mean. You're not usually such a namby-pamby. There's more to the story. Look, if you can't tell your best friend, who can you tell?"

Rochelle blew out a deep breath. "You're right. I've been going it alone for so long, I forgot what it's like to have support." She pulled her hands from Claire's grasp and laced her fingers. "Irwin hasn't said anything, but I think he regrets our marriage. I'm a terrible housewife. I told you about the cooking, and I'd rather read than clean, so the house is often a mess. Our laundry stacks up because I wash all week at work and can't face the chore when I get home."

"Irwin didn't marry you for your homemaking abilities. He loves you. Surely, he understands that you're loathe to do chores on your one day off."

"He doesn't complain, if that's what you mean."

"Look me in the eye, and tell me this is about not getting the "Housewife of the Year Award." Claire cocked her head and lifted Rochelle's chin with her index finger.

Rochelle's gaze slid to the floor, and her shoulders slumped. "Ha, ha. No, but it's just one more way I've disappointed Irwin."

Claire crossed her arms. "I'll wait as long as it takes for you to decide to tell me what's got you so upset. And if Irwin has hurt you, I'll give him what for."

"He hasn't done anything. I mean, he's been distant, but it's not like he's critical or we've fought about things. It was an arranged marriage. Maybe he's changed his mind. Maybe he's found someone else." She swiped at her falling tears. "I wouldn't blame him. I haven't been able to get pregnant. He probably wants a wife who can give him children. I know his father wants grandchildren. He's made that perfectly clear on several occasions."

"Shame on him. It's none of the old man's business whether you and Irwin have kids."

"Try telling him."

"Okay, I will."

Rochelle held up her hands in surrender. "No need for that. I want to raise a family. Why won't God give us children? Have I done something wrong? Is there a sin in my life preventing me from deserving this blessing?"

"No, no, no. I'm not convinced God punishes us like that. It just might not be his timing for you yet." Claire cleared her throat. "Have you been to the doctor? More importantly, have you discussed the topic with Irwin to see how he feels?"

"No to both questions. I'm not sure I want to know if there's something wrong with me. If I don't have the answer, I can always hope."

"Irwin could be the problem. You should both see a physician."

Rochelle swallowed past the lump in her throat. "No, it couldn't possibly be him. Maybe I should offer Irwin a divorce, so he can find a woman who will give him a family."

Chapter Fourteen

Irwin fumbled amid the coins in his pocket for his keys. Extracting them, he dropped them on the wooden floor where they landed with a jangle. He'd walked the mile from Shady Hills to the married-housing units, and his shirt stuck to his back. Perspiration gathered on his upper lip. Not exactly the way he wanted to greet Rochelle on their anniversary. She would probably look as fresh as a bouquet of freshly picked wildflowers.

He brushed his hands on his slacks and rotated his neck to ease the stiffness, then unlocked the door to let himself in. The puny apartment wasn't much, but it was home. When would the war end so he could provide Rochelle with a house she deserved? Not necessarily one as large as Father's, but something that wasn't crowded when two people stood side by side.

The knob turned under his hand, and the door swung open. A statuesque brunette with hair swept into victory rolls gaped at him. She narrowed her eyes then tossed a quick glance at Rochelle before extending her hand. "You must be Irwin. I'm Claire Porter. A *good* friend of Rochelle's."

"Nice to meet you." Irwin shook her hand. What is up with her? She didn't know him, yet she seemed to look at him with suspicion and another emotion he couldn't peg. "Uh, will you be joining us for dinner?" Please say no.

"Nope. I'm on my way out, but I'll be back." She hugged Rochelle then brushed past him with a waggle of her fingers. "Happy anniversary, you two."

Irwin closed the door and gestured to his clothing. "I would hug you too, but I don't want my sweaty clothes to dirty your outfit. Let me wash first."

"Sure." She nibbled her lower lip, a sure sign she was upset.

He'd only been home for a few moments. Had he managed to do something wrong already? Striding into the bedroom, he grabbed clean clothes and headed to the bathroom where he made quick work of washing off the day's dust, sweat, and stress.

Combing his hair he inspected his reflection in the mirror. Dark half-moons hung below his bloodshot eyes. Normally thin, his face seemed even more angular than usual. "You look terrible, old man. What does Rochelle see in you?"

A soft tap sounded behind him. "Is everything all right, Irwin?"

"Copacetic, honey. I'll be right there." He leaned close to the mirror and whispered, "Get your act together. You're supposed to be celebrating." He tossed the towel on the sink, then after a second thought, folded the cloth and hung it on the rod.

Entering the area that served as their living room, he drew Rochelle into a tight embrace then lowered his lips to hers for a kiss. Her body stiffened, and he released her. He jammed his hands into his front pockets and stepped back. "I'm sorry I had to work on our anniversary. I would have liked to have taken you somewhere nice to commemorate our big day."

"It's okay. We can go out the next time our days off coincide. Everything seems to be about the war, doesn't it? No one gets special treatment. I guess we're no different." She gestured toward the kitchen with a limp arm. "I made dinner, but it won't be ready for another few minutes or so."

He studied her, standing near the couch, arms crossed. Would she tell him what was wrong if he asked her flat out? A sigh escaped, and he pressed his lips together. He dropped onto the sofa and patted the cushion beside him. "If there's nothing you need to do to finish preparing the meal, how about if you sit and tell me about your day? You must have had a swell time with your friend. What's her name? Connie?"

Rochelle hesitated then dropped onto the couch. "Claire. She's my best friend from home. I didn't know she was coming." Her face lit up. "It was wonderful to see her. Her visit made the world disappear for a while. We talked about everything and nothing."

"That's what friends are for. I'm glad she came. Why is she here?"

"She has an interview for a job."

"At Shady Hills? You must be thrilled."

"I probably wouldn't see her much." Rochelle plucked at her skirt. "She's more intelligent than I am, so they won't assign her to the laundry room. She'd work in the office or somewhere like that."

Irwin stroked Rochelle's arm then cradled her small, delicate hands in his calloused palm. She shivered, and he searched her face. Why was she so standoffish? "Honey, you're a smart cookie. Don't denigrate yourself. The administrators will put Claire where she's needed most. With any luck that will be with you. Wouldn't it be fun to work with her? Every day would be a hen party."

The corner of her mouth lifted, but she remained mute.

"We could pray about it, if you like—"

The timer trilled, its shriek cutting across his words.

Rochelle rose, her face stiff. "That will be dinner. I scrounged up a pair of candles from one of the other married couples, and there are matches on the table. I'll take care of the food."

"You've thought of everything, haven't you? See? Claire has nothing on you."

She shrugged and hurried to the stove.

He watched her retreating back for a moment then lit the candle stubs before blowing out the match, its sharp, sulphuric smell filling the kitchen. He dropped the smoking stick into the sink. Would she ever tell him what was bothering her?

Behind him, Rochelle cried out.

He whirled as she slammed the oven door and threw the potholders onto the counter.

Her face crumpled, and she began to sob.

"What's wrong? Did you burn yourself? Are you okay?"

She shook her head continuing to weep.

Irwin wrapped his arms around her and pulled her to him. She balked, then collapsed against him, her tears wetting his shirt. He stroked her silky hair and murmured into her ear. His heart pounded. Why was she so distraught? Was she ill? Had something terrible happened that she didn't have the nerve to tell him? *Please, God, comfort her and prepare me for whatever comes.*

Minutes passed, and Rochelle quieted. She whimpered then pulled away, her head down. Shoulders sagging, she untied her apron and draped it on one of the ladder back chairs.

"Rochelle?" Irwin extended his handkerchief.

She refused to look at him but took the cloth and mopped her face.

"Rochelle, please tell me what's wrong. I'm worried about you."

Her lower lip trembled, and tears began to fall again. "I forgot to turn on the oven, so the dinner is still raw. The butcher set aside a piece of beef for us because of our anniversary, and now we may not be able to eat it because of how long it's been out of the icebox. I'm so stupid, no good at being a wife. You should never have married me. You wouldn't have if it weren't for your father. I asked Claire if I should offer you a divorce."

His breath caught, and his heart skittered. *Dear God, no!* "You want to divorce me? What did she say?"

Rochelle shook her head and pressed the handkerchief to her lips.

Irwin brushed Rochelle's hair from her face and ran his finger along her cheek. "Listen to me. I love you. My father may have brought us together, but I chose to marry you. You are not a terrible wife. Let's consider the situation. We're working six days a week, far from home, living in cramped quarters among a lot of people who don't like us. We rarely have the same day off so haven't been able to invest in our marriage. And it's all we can do to make ends meet. Sure, there have been some rocky patches, but failing to cook my dinner is no reason to want a divorce."

"That's not it." Her voice was barely above a whisper.

"Then tell me. You seemed so grieved, but I can't help you if you won't share your burden."

Her face reddened. "We've been married for a year, but I'm not...pregnant. I've failed to give you children. That's what marriage is about, and I haven't held up my part of the bargain."

"Oh, Rochelle, where did you get the idea that children are the reason people wed?" He cupped her cheek and laid a gentle kiss on her mouth. "I believe God gave marriage to people as an extra special relationship. Sometimes He blesses the union with children, but sometimes He doesn't. And you shouldn't take all the blame." His face warmed and probably matched her pink complexion. "Perhaps the fault lies with me."

She wrestled with the handkerchief then wiped her face. A shuddering sigh rocked her body, and she shook her head.

"Please believe me when I tell you it doesn't matter that you've not conceived yet. Would I like to have a child together? Yes. Will I be happy with you if we cannot? Absolutely. We are already a family, and I will challenge anyone who says differently. Do you love me?"

"Yes, more than anything."

He laid his forehead on hers and gazed into her eyes. "Then let's hold on to that. I will lead us in prayer, as I should have already been doing as your husband, and we'll ask God to give us a child. Then we'll rest in His will for us, waiting to see how He works out our request. I don't want to discount Him allowing you to get pregnant, but there are other ways to grow our family. Perhaps He will send us a war orphan or two."

May, 1945, nine months later

Chapter Fifteen

Rochelle rubbed her swollen belly as she struggled to sit up in bed. She swung her legs down and poked her feet into the slippers Claire had made for her as a birthday gift. Shuffling to the bathroom, she placed her hands in the small of her back. The doctor promised the baby could come any time, and the birth would be none too soon. Her back ached, and she hadn't seen her swollen ankles in weeks.

Because of her pregnancy, she qualified for extra rations; good for her and the baby according to all the mothers at Shady Hills. But the extra weight made her feel ungainly and ugly, so she didn't look in the mirror if it could be avoided. Irwin claimed she was lovelier than the day he married her.

She smiled. There had been bumps in the road, but she no longer doubted his love for her. Their marriage was truly blessed, and now that a child was on the way, life was even sweeter. Today marked exactly nine months since they'd beseeched God for a family. He must have answered their prayer that very night. *Thank you, Father.*

Finished with her morning preparations, Rochelle padded into the kitchen and set the filled kettle on the stove. She lit the burner then busied herself gathering dishes and silverware. Having exhausted their coffee ration for the month several days ago, she rummaged inside the tin canister that held a small supply of tea bags and selected a pair. She slid slices of bread in the toaster then set the timer. Forgetful these days, she didn't want to scorch the toast like she'd done last week.

She lowered herself onto one of the wooden, ladder-back chairs, the only seating in the house she could get in and out of without assistance. Yesterday's newspaper still lay on the kitchen table. Rochelle traced the headlines that trumpeted "NAZIS SURRENDER. WAR IN EUROPE OVER." How long before the Japanese gave up? How long before she and Irwin could return to his home and see his family?

The bedroom door opened, and Irwin emerged dressed for work, looking fresh and crisp. His face brightened, and he hurried to her. He leaned down and brushed a kiss across her lips, then knelt by her side. "How are you this morning?"

"Big as an elephant and half as agile."

He stroked her hair and chuckled. "Oh, my sweet thing, I'm sorry you're so miserable. It can't be long now, right?"

She blew out a loud breath. "I certainly hope not, although I'm nervous about what to expect. Some of the ladies have been rather…uh…enthusiastic about sharing their childbirth experiences. Will I be able to handle the pain? What if something goes wrong?"

"I will pray for you through the ordeal, that God will give you strength and that everything will be all right for you and our baby. I'm choosing to trust He wouldn't have brought us this far only to take our child."

"You're faith is so strong. I wish I could be as faithful." She frowned and laced her fingers with his. "I've been a bundle of insecurities during this pregnancy. He must get tired of me asking for peace and forgiveness for my anxiety."

"He never tires of hearing from His children."

The timer pinged, and the kettle shrieked. He rose and patted her arm. "Let me finish fixing breakfast." He flipped the toast then poured steaming water into the cups.

A cramp gripped Rochelle's stomach, and she cried out. Bent over the pain, she rubbed her side where the skin had drawn taut under her nightgown.

Irwin slammed the pot down on the burner and pivoted. He wrapped his arm around her shoulder, his eyes wide. "It's time, isn't it?"

Her muscles loosened, and Rochelle sighed. She closed her eyes and nodded. "We have to start timing the contractions. When they're five minutes apart, then we can go to the infirmary. The doctor says first babies can take a long time to come. Run down the hall and ask Mrs. Delinsky to come stay with me so you can go to work."

He gaze shot back and forth between her and the door, his eyebrows pulled together in concern. "I can't leave you."

She chuckled. "The baby isn't going to arrive after one contraction. I'll be fine."

"If you're sure…"

"Yes!"

He bolted out the door, his feet galloping down the hallway.

She smiled to herself. So much for his calm demeanor.

A second contraction seized her, and her gaze sought the clock. If she wasn't mistaken, only three minutes had passed.

Irwin paced the hallway, the sound of his leather soles slapping against the tiled floor. On his return circuit he glanced at the large clock that hung on the wall near the nurses station. Four hours since Rochelle had disappeared behind the swinging doors that led to the examination and delivery rooms, and two since the nurse had informed him the child was breech. *Lord, please don't take my family from me.*

Lester burst through the entrance, his face wreathed in smiles. "How is our lass doing?"

"Not good. The baby isn't positioned correctly." Irwin jerked his head toward the woman behind the desk bent over a stack of paper. "And the last time I asked for an update, the nurse told me it would be a while."

He raked his fingers through his hair. "I don't know how much more of this waiting I can take."

"Well, I've arranged for Harry to cover the second half of my shift, so I can keep you company. How does that sound?"

"You're a good friend, Lester." Irwin rubbed at the tightness in his chest. "What if…" He couldn't bear to finish the sentence.

Lester gripped Irwin's shoulders. "Let's storm the gates of heaven for our gal, shall we?" He grinned. "And for you, too. You're completely knackered, aren't you?"

"I am exhausted, and I hate that she has to go through so much pain and difficulty to give us a child. I wish I could undergo the experience for her."

"Now, you're talking like a true husband." He bowed his head. "Father, we're here to ask You to help this young couple traverse this part of their journey. Wrap Your loving arms around Rochelle and give her strength to bear this child, safely and as painlessly as possible. Be with Irwin and give him Your peace that passes all understanding. Thank You for blessing this little family with new life. In the name of Your Son, Jesus. Amen."

Another hour passed. Irwin stared at the large clock on the wall. His stomach clenched. Each minute seemed to last an eternity. He blew out a loud breath and scrubbed at his face with cold fingers.

Lester squeezed his knee. "Glaring at the clock won't make it move any faster, lad. The waitin' is hard—"

Behind them, the door swung open with a bang. Footsteps approached, and Irwin turned. The doctor wore a tired smile. "Congratulations, Mr. Terrell. You're the father of two healthy boys. Your wife and the babies are fine, and you can go in to see them."

Irwin's heart hammered in his chest. "Two…I've got two sons?"

"Yes, sir." He gestured toward the doors. "First door on the left."

Lester let out a loud whoop and clapped Irwin on the back. "Twice the blessing, man. God is good, isn't He?"

Numb, Irwin nodded.

With a laugh, Lester propelled him toward the doors. "Now, go in there, and tell your wife how much you love her."

Irwin stumbled forward, then looked back at Lester and grinned. He shoved open the door and hurried through. In the small, sterile room Rochelle lay on a narrow cot, her face pale and lined with fatigue. Two tiny, identical, blanket-wrapped bundles lay in her arms. The nurse smoothed the bedcovers then nodded at him before slipping from the room.

He rushed to Rochelle's side and kissed her satiny cheek. He scooted the wooden chair close to the bed and sat. "Was it awful? I'm sorry you had to suffer through the birth, darling."

"It's over now, and we have two beautiful babies. Can you believe it, Irwin? God gave us two children in answer to our prayer. He blessed us abundantly, didn't He?"

"I was blessed from the moment you appeared. I love you, Rochelle."

She cocked her head and snickered. "You're a smooth talker, but I love you, too."

THE END

What did you think of *Love's Allegiance*?

Thank you so much for purchasing *Love's Allegiance*. You could have selected any number of books to read, but you chose this book.

I hope it added encouragement and exhortation to your life. If so, it would be nice if you could share this book with your family and friends by posting to Facebook (www.facebook.com) and/or Twitter (www.twitter.com).

If you enjoyed this book and found some benefit in reading it, I'd appreciate it if you could take some time to post a review on Amazon, Goodreads, Kobo, Google Play, Apple Books, or other book review site of your choice. Your feedback and support will help me to improve my writing craft for future projects and make this book even better.

Thank you again for your purchase.

Blessings,

Linda Shenton Matchett

Reader's Guide

1. Over 12,000 conscientious objectors served during WWII. This is an often overlooked aspect of the war. Were you aware of it? Do you agree or disagree with conscientious objection. Why?
2. Some conscientious objectors volunteered to be guinea pigs in one of the dangerous and life-threatening medical studies conducted by medical colleges and universities on behalf of the U.S. government (e.g., effects of starvation, finding cures for malaria, typhus, hepatitis, etc.) Were you aware of these programs? How do you feel about people volunteering in this capacity?
3. Irwin chooses to serve in a mental hospital. At this time most treatments included electric shock, restraint (a straitjacket or being tied to a bed), and corporal punishment. The scene where Irwin uses calm words, offering to hold the patient's hand, and take him for a walk is based on a real incident. Did you find it realistic? Do you think all mental illness is curable? Or is there "no hope" for some?
4. Rochelle leaves everything she knows and agrees to a trial "courtship" with a man she's never met. How is this similar to online dating? Dissimilar? Would you be willing to do what Rochelle did?
5. Lester sticks by Irwin even after he accuses Lester of wrongdoing? Would you have been able to be that kind of friend? Do you have a friend like that?
6. Mrs. Harridan takes out her worry for her son on Rochelle and Irwin by treating them poorly. Rochelle addresses the situation with Mrs. Harridan. Do you think Rochelle did a good job of handling the situation? What would you have done differently? Have you ever experienced something like this?
7. There are several secondary characters. Are there any who stand out to you? What was it about them that attracted you to them?
8. How did you feel about the spirituality in the characters' lives? Are there specific characters whose faith resonates with yours?

9. Think about ways *Love's Allegiance* points to better things to come through Jesus Christ.
10. What lessons from this story can you apply to your own life?

Historical Background

Dear Reader:

I hope you enjoyed *Love's Allegiance*, inspired by the biblical story of Rebekkah (also spelled Rebekah) and Isaac. Please consider reading the original story found in the twenty-fourth chapter of Genesis.

Many books, both fiction and non-fiction, have been written about the combat and home front aspects of WWII. There are a number of memoirs, autobiographies, and books published by and about the conscientious objectors who served in various capacities during that time. However, I didn't find any novels that explored the COs' side of the war and decided that melding Rebekkah and Isaac's story with that of the "peace churches" would make for interesting reading. I hope you agree.

Here's a bit of background about the history of conscientious objection in the United States:

During the colonial era, exemptions to military service were allowed for members of pacifist religious groups. When the Civil War broke out, the federal government also recognized conscientious objectors (CO). In WWI, laws changed and restrictions were placed on COs, resulting in many men going to prison. Countless COs served as medics during WWII, but a large number felt that entering the military, even in noncombatant roles, violated their beliefs. Fortunately for them, the government devised a program of "alternative civilian service."

Called the Civilian Public Service, the program was jointly created by the Selective Service Department and a committee of representatives from the peace churches, such as the Mennonites, Religious Society of Friends (Quakers), Church of the Brethren, Amish, and others. Conscientious Objectors were (and still are) required to register with the Selective Service. During WWII, after their status was confirmed, the men were assigned to CPS camps where they performed soil conservation, firefighting, agricultural tasks, and maintenance of national parks. Feeling that many of the jobs were "make-work," some of the COs applied to serve in mental health hospitals or for acceptance into one of the dangerous and life-threatening medical studies conducted by various medical colleges on behalf of the government.

CPS employees were unpaid and received very little support from the government. Instead, the men were provided for by their families and home churches. Between 1941 and 1947, over 12,000 conscientious objectors served around the world.

Acknowledgments

Although writing a book is a solitary task, it is not a solitary journey. There have been many who have helped and encouraged me along the way.

My parents, Richard and Jean Shenton, who presented me with my first writing tablet and encouraged me to capture my imagination with words. Thanks, Mom and Dad!

Scribes212 – my ACFW online critique group: Valerie Goree, Marcia Lahti, and the late Loretta Boyett (passed on to Glory, but never forgotten). Without your input, my writing would not be nearly as effective.

Eva Marie Everson – my mentor/instructor with Christian Writers' Guild. You took a timid, untrained student and turned her into a writer. Many thanks!

SincNE, and the folks who coordinate the Crimebake Writing Conference. I have attended many writing conferences, but without a doubt, Crimebake is one of the best. The workshops, seminars, panels, critiques, and every tiny aspect are well-executed, professional, and educational.

Special thanks to Hank Phillippi Ryan, Halle Ephron, and Roberta Isleib for your encouragement and spot-on critiques of my work.

Paula Proofreader (https://paulaproofreader.wixsite.com/home): I'm so glad I found you! My work is cleaner because of your eagle eye. Any mistakes are completely mine.

Research is an integral part of any book, and I was fortunate to receive lots of help along the way. Thanks to Jeff Kelliher, Communications & Media

Relations Manager at Brattleboro Retreat, who gave me an extensive behind-the-scenes tour of the facility and answered my countless questions. The retreat, now a psychiatric and addiction treatment center, operated as a mental hospital where conscientious objectors served during WWII. You can learn more about the important work the Retreat does by visiting their website: http://www.brattlebororetreat.org.

Much appreciation goes to Sisters in Crime New England Chapter President Connie Johnson Hambley who spent time with me on the telephone, even though she was dealing with a family situation, to coach me about the ins and outs of horses and horseback riding. We only scratched the surface of the topic, but I'm hopeful that her comprehensive knowledge and plot suggestions made *Love's Allegiance* richer for her assistance. Any errors are my own.

Thanks to my Book Brigade who provide information, encouragement, and support.

A heartfelt thank you to my brothers, Jack Shenton and Douglas Shenton, and my sister, Susan Shenton Greger for being enthusiastic cheerleaders during my writing journey. Your support means more than you'll know.

My husband, Wes, deserves special kudos for understanding my need to write. Thank you for creating my writing room—it's perfect, and I'm thankful for it every day. Thank you for your willingness to accept a house that's a bit cluttered, laundry that's not always done, and meals on the go. I love you.

And finally, to God be the glory. I thank Him for giving me the gift of writing and the inspiration to tell stories that shine the light on His goodness and mercy.

Other Titles

Romance

Love's Harvest, Wartime Brides, Book 1

Love's Rescue, Wartime Brides, Book 2

Love's Belief, Wartime Brides, Book 3

Love Found in Sherwood Forest

On the Rails

A Love Not Forgotten (Let Love Spring Collection)

A Doctor in the House (The Hope of Christmas Collection)

Mystery

Under Fire

Murder of Convenience, Women of Courage, Book 1

Non-Fiction

WWII Word Find, Volume 1

WWII Bits and Pieces

Let's Connect!

www.LindaShentonMatchett.com

www.facebook.com/LindaShentonMatchettAuthor

www.twitter.com/lindasmatchett

www.pinterest.com/lindasmatchett

www.linkedin.com/in/authorlindamatchett

https://www.amazon.com/Linda-Shenton-Matchett/e/B01DNB54S0

Sign up for my newsletter and receive a FREE short story

https://bit.ly/2MXJFgC

Interested in more historical fiction?

Visit http://www.lindashentonmatchett.com/p/books.html

www.ingramcontent.com/pod-product-compliance
Lightning Source LLC
Chambersburg PA
CBHW021020120726
47905CB00009B/3107